The Keeper of the Isis Light

THE KEEPER OF
THE ISIS LIGHT

Monica Hughes

AN ARGO BOOK

ATHENEUM *1984* NEW YORK

LIBRARY OF CONGRESS CATALOGING IN PUBLICATION DATA

Hughes, Monica.
The keeper of the Isis light.

"An Argo book."
Summary: Sixteen-year-old Olwen, who lives alone
on the planet Isis with her faithful robot, falls
in love with an arrival from earth
and complications ensue.
[1. Science fiction] I. Title
PZ7.87364Ke 1981   [Fic]   81-1340
ISBN 0-689-30847-7   AACR2

First Printing July 1980
Second Printing January 1984

The Keeper of the Isis Light

Chapter One

It was a day like any other day on Isis, and yet, when it was over, nothing would ever be the same again. Olwen scrambled up the rocky eastern face of Lighthouse Mesa, her hands and feet moving instinctively from foothold to crack. In the worst places Guardian had lasered out steps, so that from their house, halfway up the cliff, the path was like a crude stone ladder.

She pulled herself over the verge and dropped down onto the wiry grass, breathing in deep lungfulls of the thin, sharp air. When she lay on her back there was nothing but sky, a clear dome of intense blue-green that gave her a feeling inside that was half joy, half pain. Ra was high in the sky, nearly at ten hours, and she shut her eyes against its intense white light.

After a while it got uncomfortably hot, and she unzipped her light jumpsuit and baked her naked skin in the sun. Summer was coming at last. She could feel a real bite in Ra's rays today. She rolled over and felt the heat go right through her skin and into her spine. She sighed and stretched, and dreamed.

Today was her birthday, her tenth year on Isis. Guardian had explained that according to Earth reckoning she would be sixteen, but here, on wide-orbiting Isis, it was her tenth birthday. What had Guardian planned? Every year there was a surprise. He was delightfully thoughtful and inventive, and this morning he had practically pushed her out of the house and told her not to come home until supper-time. So something was being planned.

She was too excited to lie still any longer. She wriggled into her jumpsuit again, after making sure that none of the

1

cactuses that dotted the mesa top had left spines in her skin. Tough though her skin was, a lodged cactus spine could cause a festering spot that would be hard to heal.

Standing on the mesa top, grey-green with stiff grass and bulbous cactuses that would soon burst into bloom, Olwen looked out over her world. To the west and north lay range after range of mountains, some jaggy-peaked, some, like Lighthouse Mesa, worn to a table-top smoothness. To the south a deep bowl of grassland separated her from another moutain range, and to the east a river drained the high north country and spilled itself down a series of watery steps that she had named the Cascades. Once the river reached the valley it slowly lost its impetus and widened into a lake surrounded by small fruit trees. They would be in bloom now, she supposed, though from this height the thickness of the atmosphere, like a smoky haze, veiled the detail from her eyes.

She never went down into the valley if she could help it. It was so much nicer up here, where the air was so clear and thin that you could see for a hundred kilometres, fold on fold of red and purple crags, shadowed black by the hard white light of Ra. Ten o'clock. Noon. Right now solar particles would be bombarding this part of Isis at maximum intensity, blotting out any signals that might come in to the Light. Not that many did. Perhaps one or two a year. The Light was chiefly designed for sending.

The communications room itself was underground, tucked away in solid rock at the very back of their cliff home; but the signals were sent from the dish-shaped antenna that stood on the top of the mesa close by. Twenty hours a day there streamed into space a beam of faster-than-light particles proclaiming that here, at co-ordinates so and so, in the elliptical three-space known as the Milky Way Galaxy, was Isis, fourth planet of the F5 star Ra, in the constellation Indus.

This message alone was sufficient to tell any passing cargo vessel that here was a planet suitable for an emergency landfall, habitable, given certain precautions; and that here a mariner in distress would find other human beings, the Keepers of the Light.

But Isis was much more than a useful rock in the sea of

space on which Man had planted a beacon. Eventually Isis would be settled, when the more "comfortable" planets within six parsecs of Earth were used up. So three times a day, at dawn, at sunset and at midnight, the Guardian would stop whatever he was doing to beam a signal back towards Earth—a weather report, a log of events since the previous signal, and a personal report from herself, Olwen Pendennis.

Sometimes Olwen felt stupid about her report. Why would anybody parsecs away on Earth be interested in what she ate for breakfast, how she was doing in celestial mechanics, what she felt about life in general? But Guardian had said that the report was essential. Ever since she had been old enough to talk intelligently she had had to give it. That was why she was here on Isis. If her report were not completely essential then Guardian alone would be here, doing the things he did best, weather, seismic, geological reports, lists of flora and fauna.

Where would she be then? On Earth, perhaps, elbow to elbow with people . . . She looked around her at the purple and orange mountains, at the silvery-grey grass, at the empty sky, and she stretched out her arms as if she could embrace the whole world. Oh, how lucky she was, to have a whole beautiful planet to herself. Just her and Guardian . . .

A wild baying sound echoed up from the valley close to the Cascades, and she laughed. And Hobbit, too, she remembered. She had almost forgotten Hobbit, and that wouldn't do at all. She ran close to the edge of the cliff, her eyes slit against the light bouncing off the rocks, and peered down into the giddy depths. There was a movement among the thorn bushes about half way down, and she glimpsed the flurry of a plumed tail. She leaned perilously over the edge and gave a piercing whistle.

At once the tail stiffened, a long nose came up quivering, and as she whistled again the creature came bounding up the stone ladder to the mesa top, flung itself at Olwen and began to lick her enthusiastically.

Even though she had been ready for him, the weight of his huge paws against her chest sent her staggering backwards, to catch her bare heel against a rock and land with a whump on a patch of wiry grass, luckily not among the cactuses. Hobbit licked her frantically and then, as if he had suddenly forgotten what all the fuss was about, collapsed on his side, his great tongue lolling out of his tooth-filled mouth.

Olwen wriggled until her head was propped against Hobbit's heaving side, and lay comfortably sprawled, eyes half shut. Even behind her closed lids Ra was still intensely bright, and when she looked into the shadows she could see nothing but dancing violet-coloured sunspots.

She turned on her side. In the crevices between rocks pockets of soil had collected and tiny plants grew, jewel-like flowers, smaller than her little finger-nail, borne on hair-slender stems. Their minute leaves had water-gathering cells that shone in the sun like carved crystals. Among their spidery roots ran insects—the equivalent of insects, for they were far different from Earth's—many-legged creatures with brilliant wing-cases, striped and spotted, every colour of the rainbow. Olwen dozed after a while, comfortably propped against Hobbit's furry side.

She was wakened by the insistent beep of her wrist communicator. She yawned herself awake and sat up, blinking. "Hullo?"

"What were you doing? I beeped for thirteen seconds before you answered."

"Sorry, Guardian. I'm up on the mesa. I must have fallen asleep. The sun's almost setting. I've been asleep for hours."

"Up on the mesa? That was unwise, my dear. You might get burned."

"Oh, my skin's far too tough to sunburn. What was it? Do you want me for anything special?" she asked casually, holding back a giggle. Guardian's surprises were always so deliciously ponderous.

"Yes. Would you return to the house, please, Olwen."

"It's lovely up here. Is it important?" She loved to tease him. He was always so solemn, and such a rotten liar.

"Yes. Ah . . . I thought this would be a good time to check your measurements. You may need some new summer clothes."

"Oh, I'm sure the stuff you made for me last year will still fit," she said casually.

Pause. Then, "Nevertheless, I should like to be sure."

4

"All right." She did laugh then. "I'm coming right down. May I bring Hobbit?"

"*Not* in the house." Guardian's voice was firm.

"But his feelings are so hurt when I make him stay on the terrace. *Please*, Guardian."

"Absolutely not. And *Draco Hirsutus* does not have feelings."

"Hobbit does," she contradicted him. "Oh, all right. I won't tease. I'm coming down right now." She plunged down the dizzy stone ladder, fingers and toes clinging to the holds.

About halfway down the cliff a natural horizontal fault had been deepened to make a terrace three metres wide and ten metres long. A low balustrade of natural rock had been left at its edge, and there were bamboo chairs and tables, and a sort of hammock suspended in the shade of the rocky overhang.

At the corners of the terrace there were flowering shrubs in pots, shrubs that came from the other side of the continent, by the far sea. Guardian had brought them back for her birthday two years ago, and on the shady terrace, with daily watering, they flourished and bloomed all year round.

Behind the terrace, carved out of the rock of the mesa itself, were two large high-ceilinged rooms with windows in the east wall. One of these was Olwen's own room. She and Guardian had had a lot of fun decorating it together. Neither of them had a very clear idea of what a young girl's bedroom should be like, but Guardian had recalled old memories and invented new fabrics, and Olwen loved the result.

The second room was the living room, library, and everything else in one. In summer Olwen had most of her meals out on the terrace, with the soft wind and the sound of the Cascades below; but in winter, or when the equinoctial gales tore down from the mountains to the north, she ate at a small table drawn up before the living room fire.

The books, the music and learning tapes, and a few small precious ornaments had come to Isis with the original landing party, Guardian had once told her, when Olwen had asked him if he had made everything that was theirs. She had to take his word for that. She had no recollection of any of the early years on Isis. Memory began for her . . . when was

5

it? She counted back the birthdays.

Nine. On her ninth birthday Guardian had made a set of jewellery for her, set with fire-stones from the far northern mountains. On her eighth birthday he had brought back the flowering shrubs. When she was seven . . . she stood by the terrace door, frowning in an effort to remember . . . of course! That was the year Guardian had found Hobbit. He had been just a pup then, of course, only half a metre long and cuddly. She grinned at the memory of Guardian's face when he realised just how huge Hobbit was going to grow.

Her sixth year was the one in which they had transformed her room from a nursery playroom to its present elegance. Five . . . Five was the year that she learned how to paint, and Guardian had made a wonderful box of colours for her, and sheets of paper and boards.

Four. When she was four there had been the dolls' house, complete with a family of father, mother, two children and a baby. She suddenly remembered, as if it had only just happened, that she had turned from her play to ask Guardian, "Why don't I have a mother and father too?"

He had answered in his soft voice, "Don't you remember, Olwen? I am your father and mother." After that she had played with the dolls' house most contently for hours at a time.

The memory was so clear that she felt she could reach out and touch that other Olwen. Why then could she remember no further back? Three? She thought about being three until her head was whirling, but there was nothing there at all, not even the smallest hint. It was not like looking down into the valley mists, where the details were hidden in a vague shimmer of colour. It was more as if there was nothing back there to hide. Just emptiness. Non-existence.

To be three years old on Isis would be just the same as being five years old on Earth, she worked out. She had read lots of books and tapes about Earth. Five-year-old girls were already going to school, so they could certainly remember further back in their lives than that.

"Olwen!" Guardian's voice came from inside the house.

She started. "Oh! Coming." She patted Hobbit's head and pushed his eager muzzle aside, forcing him to stay out on the terrace.

The living room was empty, and Guardian's voice called from the kitchen. "I will have tea ready in about ten minutes. How about changing first?"

"Yes. I'll try not to be too long, but I must have a shower first. I'm all hot and sticky."

"You *did* get a sunburn!"

"Honestly, no. Don't fuss, Guardian dear. I won't be long." She ran across the stone floor of the living room and into her own room. Since her sixth birthday and the redecorating she and Guardian had made a bargain. She was to keep her room clean and tidy and he was to stay out. So, just for a second, annoyance bubbled up inside her when she stopped on the threshold and realised that something had been changed. Then she blinked and stared and . . . "Wow! Oh, wow!"

She rushed across to the frilled and canopied bed. On the counterpane was laid out a long dress of gold lamé stuff, and on the bedside rug was a pair of elegant golden sandals. "Wow!" she yelled again, and tore off her jumpsuit and shot into the shower.

Five minutes later she reverently lifted the gorgeous dress and dropped it over her head. It fitted perfectly, of course. Everything Guardian attempted turned out absolutely perfect—sometimes it was hard to live up to. She slipped her feet into the sandals and looked down at the shining length of herself, stroking the fabric lovingly. A quick brush of her thick reddish-brown hair and she was ready.

The high heels and the tight-fitting sheath forced her to walk in a brand-new fashion, with small steps, so that her hips moved. She had never felt so . . . so different, so grown-up, in her whole life. Then, as she began to walk, she found that Guardian had not finished with surprises. In some fashion he had built a kind of music into the fibres of the fabric, so that now that it was warm with her body heat it vibrated, a gentle humming when she moved slowly, a music like the sound of harps when she walked fast.

"Oh, Guardian!" She whirled out of her room, spinning faster and faster until she was wrapped around in arpeggios and cadenzas, and finally her high heels caught in the edge of one of the living room rugs and she fell into a chair, her laughter mixing with the dying fall of the music.

Guardian stood, looking very correct and official, by the little table, which he had drawn close to one of the big windows which looked down upon the chasm and the Cascades. There was a hint of a smile upon his normally sober face. She scrambled up and ran—carefully—to him, the music spinning out behind her. "Thank you, thank you a million times, dear Guardian. It's the most scrumptious gorgeous dress in the whole galaxy and I love it!" She threw her arms around his neck and kissed his cheek.

"Happy tenth birthday, Olwen, my dear," he said, and held the chair back for her to sit down.

"Oh, it all looks super. Marvellous. What a lovely surprise!" Her eyes took in the silver, the best Earth-style china, for special occasions only, the dishes full of all the things that she'd ever said she'd loved—and she was a girl of enormous enthusiasms, and Guardian's memory was infallible. I'll never eat the half of it, she thought, swallowing a giggle at Guardian's extravagence.

In the exact centre of the laden table was the cake, a monument filigreed over with silver and spun sugar, with ten candles burning at its summit. Guardian had even made a special birthday tape for her, by singing over and over again in different voices, so that when he switched it on the room was quite filled with a chorus of voices: 'Happy Birthday, dear Olwen, happy birthday to you. . .'

"It's the nicest thing you've ever done for me. Darling Guardian, thank you."

He smiled down at her, and gently moved a lock of hair that had tossed itself over to the wrong side of her parting in her wild dance. "I'll pour your tea, shall I?"

"That would be lovely. My goodness, I'm starving!" She took a deep breath and began to dig into the delicacies in front of her.

"Aren't you going to wish? The candles will not burn for ever."

"I forgot. Oh, Guardian, what am I going to wish for? I've got everything I want, absolutely everything . . . I know! I wish that everything will go on being perfect, just

8

the way it is now." She took a deep breath and blew. Nine candles went out obediently. The tenth flickered, sent up a shower of sparks and glowed on for a moment before giving up. "Oh, dear. I hope that still counts."

"I am sure it does. You did extinguish them all in the one breath."

When Olwen had finished eating, more than was actually comfortable, just for the joy of seeing the pleasure on Guardian's face as he watched her demolish his handiwork, she collapsed into one of the big chairs with a sigh. "If I'm not careful I'll grow too big for this gorgeous dress."

"If you do I will just let it out or make you another," said Guardian calmly. He sat down beside her and put his arm around her shoulder.

"What a comfort you are." She snuggled against his shoulder, hearing the aliveness of him through the tunic he always wore. He had programmed an evening of chamber music, and they listened in peaceful silence for a while.

Then, "You wished that everything would go on being the same for ever, Olwen. That was not a very wise wish."

"I don't care. If everything is perfect why would one ever want it to change?"

"Stasis is death" Guardian quoted. "Do you understand what that means?"

"I understand what you're saying, but I don't see why it has to be so. Look at this evening." She waved her arm towards the window, and her dress chimed a cadenza. The sky had darkened to a deep blue-green, against which the eastern mountains and the Cascades were silhouetted. In the very last of the light the falling water was like quicksilver. There was no breeze, and outside nothing stirred. "Look at it, Guardian. Perfect."

"But it is changing even while you watch, Olwen. Soon the stars will be out. Ra is excitable this week, so later the northern lights will put on a display for you. Would you forgo that to keep this? Then in ten hours it will be daylight again. Somewhere a cactus will bloom for the first time this year. Down in the valley the fruit trees are already in flower. Would you wish them to stay that way forever, giving you no fruit?"

"No. No, of course not." Olwen hesitated. "That's not the kind of change I mean. Those are just little things. I mean you and me."

"If you and I ceased to exist tonight it would make no difference to Isis. And Ra would still rise in the morning. The galaxy would go on without us."

"Yes, but . . ." Olwen laughed, half vexed, half amused. Arguing with Guardian was so difficult. Sometimes, dear though he was, he seemed to have a viewpoint parsecs away from hers. "All I really meant was that I wanted nothing ever to change between you and me. And Hobbit. I want the three of us to go on being happy, as happy as today, for ever."

Guardian nodded, but did not reply. When he spoke it was to change the subject. "Did you enjoy your birthday music?"

She thought about it, head on one side. "It was different. You've never done anything like that before, have you? It was as if . . . well, as if the room were filled with people. Funny. I'm not sure that I like that idea."

"They were all singing best wishes to you."

"I know, but it was just pretend, of course. I wonder what it would really be like to have a party with other people there. I don't know. No, I don't think so. I don't want anyone else but you, Guardian dear. You're perfect. But why are you asking things like this? Are you worried about me or something? I'll sit in your silly chair and let you take a psychological profile of me if you want. If it'll make you feel better. But, honestly, I'm absolutely and completely happy."

The concerto ended in a final triumphant flourish of violin and cello. The room was silent. Outside the windows night flooded the chasm and began to spill over the terrace. Beyond the north-eastern mountains the northern lights began to glow, flickering in shots of hot red, shimmering like green silk curtains.

"Will you put on another music tape, Guardian?"

"There is something else I want you to hear first, Olwen, something new."

"What is it?"

"An incoming signal."

"Picked up by the Light?" Olwen sprang to her feet in a

10

swirl of gold. "A cargo vessel? Passing by or landing? Oh, I can tell by your face that it's going to land. Oh, how exciting! Why didn't you tell me sooner? I wonder what they'll have on board. New books perhaps. Or music. I hope they'll want to barter us some things for fire-stones. Oh, Guardian, it's so thrilling! Is this what you've been leading up to with your funny questions? As if I'd mind a cargo vessel landing here! Oh, I will get to meet them this time, won't I? There won't be any stupid quarantine regulations, will there? I remember the last time a cargo ship stopped here. Years and years ago, it was. But you wouldn't let me meet them. This time it'll be different, won't it . . ."

"Olwen!" Guardian's voice broke through her excited chatter. Something unfamiliar in the tone stopped her cold. She stared at him. "Olwen, it is *not* a cargo vessel. It's a passenger ship. One of S.T.C.'s."

"The Stellar Travel Consortium? But that's the line we came to Isis on." Olwen felt a cold lump in the pit of her stomach. "Oh, Guardian, they're not coming to take us away from Isis, are they? They're not going to close down the Light? I won't go. I simply won't go. I'd run away first!"

"Easy, Olwen. Do not get so stirred up. If you would only stop talking long enough for me to explain, it will really be much simpler. The ship that is arriving is a settlers' ship."

"Bound for . . .?"

"For here, Olwen. For Isis."

"No!"

"Do not look so shocked. You know that we are designated as a Class B-One planet. The emigration authorities back on Earth must have run out of comfortably close Class A planets, and our name has come up. There will be a full pioneer settlement coming in, eighty people, men, women and children."

"To live here? For ever? On *our* planet?"

Guardian nodded, his eyes on her face. Olwen turned away. When she spoke next her voice was muffled. "What happens to *us*?"

"Nothing new. You know the Light-Keeper's Code as well as I do. To maintain the Light at all times, and to render all due assistance to mariners in distress and to duly

11

authorized settlers."

Olwen stamped her foot. "But I don't want to . . ."

"I am sorry, my dear. That is not important any more." Guardian's voice was gentle, but firm, and she stared at him disbelievingly. She opened her mouth, but couldn't think of a thing to say. She stared wildly round the cosy room. Behind Guardian was the table with the ruin of her birthday feast, the candles charred, one tipped rakishly like the tower of Pisa back on Earth. Outside in the night of Isis the northern lights flamed balefully.

She turned and ran to her room as fast as her high heels would let her, the sobs crowding her throat, her dress chiming happily. Guardian came after her, but stopped on the threshold.

"Olwen, please listen."

"I won't. Go away. Oh, don't you understand? It's all spoilt now."

"You must listen to the tape, Olwen. You are the Keeper of the Light. It is your duty."

"I don't care. I won't. *You* listen. *You* deal with it. I won't. Not now. Not ever." She flung herself down on her bed and glared up at the ceiling. She knew that she was behaving dreadfully, and that by tomorrow she'd probably be deeply ashamed of herself. Right now that didn't matter. The hurt feeling inside her made her want to go on behaving badly, perhaps do something completely outrageous, if she could only think of something.

Out of the corner of her eye she could see Guardian, hesitating on the threshold. For a moment she thought that he was going to come in, and she began to get extra angry in readiness. But then, with just the hint of a sigh, he went away, so she didn't even have the excuse of being angry with him.

She lay glumly and stared at the ceiling. It had originally been plain rock, like the walls and the floor, left when Guardian had carved their house out of the side of the mesa; but now pretty panels of cream and rose covered the walls, and the ceiling was of semi-transparent stuff, with lights behind it, that Guardian had made so that she could dim or brighten and even change the colour of them, just by thinking about it.

Right now her thoughts were deeply angry, and the room lights had dimmed and turned a sort of horrid dirty purple. She'd never seen them do *that* before. It made the pretty rose-coloured walls and the flowery curtains and bed-frills look truly hideous.

A sudden hissing filled the room and she sat up on the bed with an indignant bounce. Guardian had most unfairly abandoned the argument with her and put the offensive tape on the intercom—very loudly.

"That's not fair!" she yelled at the open door. The hissing died down and a voice took over, a man's voice, deep, with a warm attractive quality about it. In spite of herself she listened. And after all, it *was* very loud.

"This is the Pegasus Two calling Isis. Captain Jonas Tryon of the Pegasus Two, calling the Keeper of the Isis Light. Come in, Isis."

There was a pause, free from hissing, which must mean that Guardian had cut the tape. When the hissing began again it was still the Captain's voice.

"Landfall in two of your days, Isis. Eighty settlers aboard. Request preparations for landing, and any special instructions for the safety of my passengers. Request updated weather report . . ."

There was another pause. Olwen found herself half-wanting to hear the stranger's voice again, half-wishing he would shut up and go away.

". . . look forward to seeing you then," the tape went on chattily. Olwen thumped angrily over onto her front and put the pillow over her head. "You've been a long time alone, Isis," the tape concluded.

Chapter Two

As inevitably as Ra rose every morning and set every night, and the moons Shu and Nut raced each other across the sky, so, no matter how Olwen might rage, the STC passenger vessel, Pegasus Two, made planetfall in the centre of the grassland to the south of Lighthouse Mesa two days later.

Olwen watched it come in from the top of the mesa. It dropped out of the sky butt first, rockets flaring, close enough for her to read the remains of the identification letters on its battered side, letters sand-blasted by a five-parsec journey through interstellar dust. If the ship itself looked so worn and battered, how had its passengers survived the lengthy ordeal?

The day before the landing, Guardian had been busy from dawn until after nightfall clearing the landing site, leaving Olwen at the house to monitor incoming signals. He had cut a circular swathe of the high flowering grass a kilometre in diameter, and sprayed it thoroughly with fire-retardant. It would be a poor beginning for the settlers to burn up their new planet before ever setting foot on it.

Olwen's work was almost automatic, taping in-coming messages and sending out tapes of local data on present weather conditions, available safe foods, local predators—all the details necessary for the captain to set up a safe camp for the people under his charge. Once they had settled in, the new colonists would make their own assessments and come to their own decisions, right or wrong. But now, to begin with, exhausted and disoriented as they must be, a split-second decision wrongly made could mean the disastrous end of a colony before it had barely begun. It had happened before, on other planets, revolving around other suns.

Idly Olwen had listened to the tapes as they were transmitted. They had been compiled from data collected by both of them, and it seemed to Olwen that Guardian was being unnecessarily fussy and overprotective towards the new settlers. All that talk about the low oxygen content of the atmosphere, and the high ultra-violet radiation, due to Ra's status as an F-type star which made it noticeably hotter than Earth's sun. The new settlers had been warned to stay in the valleys and not to attempt to climb even the lower slopes of the mountains without oxygen equipment and ultra-violet-opaque suits. It was ridiculous!

Here she sat, on the highest mesa in this quadrant of Isis, enjoying the spring warmth of Ra on her naked arms and legs, and breathing the sharp clean air with enjoyment. But of course these poor settlers had come from the sticky oxygen-thick atmosphere of Earth, which had a sun, she gathered, that you could hardly warm your hands at. They were not used to Isis, that was all. As soon as they had acclimatized there would not be all this fuss about oxygen and UVO suits.

The rocket hovered. Its retro-jets thundered against the bare surface of Isis, flames flattening and fanning out along the ground. The noise rolled around the plain and ricocheted off the surrounding mountains in a harsh continuous thunder. Then suddenly the jets cut out, the ship rocked and then stood squatly still, and the silence pressed against her eardrums.

The birds had fled in coveys as the descent had begun. The grassland animals had fled too, and were lying low, the deer and the rabbits. Even up here in the safety of the mesa top, the moles and dormice had gone to earth, or curled themselves into balls, as still as the red and purple rocks they resembled.

Nothing moved anywhere. It was so still that up here, a thousand metres above the landing site, Olwen could hear the crack and pop of metal as Pegasus Two slowly cooled down from its entry into the atmosphere of Isis.

If the people aboard were to come out now, she thought, they would imagine that they had arrived on a deserted planet. Nothing happened. Nothing stirred. She sat down with her back comfortably against a rock and ate the sandwich she had brought for her lunch. After a time one of the creatures she had named tittlemice poked a twitching nose out of its burrow. The wide whiskers fanned out and the nose caught the scent of Olwen's food. It hopped from its hole and scurried across to Olwen's side and began to range to and fro, gathering up the crumbs she had dropped.

A mountain lark took flight and soared up towards Ra until it was no more than a dot in the wide sky. Then, closing its wings, it catapulted down, singing its triumphant song. It was a tiny bird, smaller than the palm of her hand. It nested among the cactuses, building a nest of grass smaller than a tea-cup, in which it usually laid four exquisite tiny purple eggs. Its song was the most beautiful sound on Isis, and yet, in some strange way Olwen could not understand, the beauty seemed to be full of pain. It left her with a strange aching emptiness in her middle, as if she lacked something terribly important, and did not even know what it was.

Which doesn't make sense, she told herself for the umpteenth time. I am happy on Isis. Perfectly, gloriously happy. Or at least I was until now. I need nobody in the whole world but Guardian, and he needs nobody but me. So why do I feel as if my heart was broken, just a little bit, every time I hear the song of the lark?

Down in the valley things were beginning to happen at last. Olwen sat cross-legged on the very edge of the southern cliff and focussed her binoculars downward. The main loading door of the ship creaked open, and a stairway extruded itself just below the opening. She stared through her glasses at the dark square in the ship's side. Even with corrective lenses it was a little like looking through a mist. She wished that the soupy atmosphere of the valley was not there to get between her and her first view of the strangers from Earth.

A tall, wide-shouldered figure in space-white suddenly filled the dark square. Captain Jonas Tryon. Olwen said the name aloud. It had a good ring. It could be the name of the captain of a Nantucket whaler, or of a tea-clipper like the Cutty Sark. She fiddled with the focus of the binoculars until the face jumped into unexpected clarity. She found her heart thudding with excitement. Oh, how different he was from

16

Guardian!

Where Guardian's face was smooth and of a delicate golden tan, this man was craggy, as craggy as the side of the mesa, with deep grooves running from nose to mouth. Even his skin was the ruddy rock colour of Isis. At this distance, through the thick atmosphere of the valley, she could see no more, but she knew instinctively that his eyes would be blue . . . mariner-blue, and far-seeing.

She could not see his face any more, as he looked down and began to descend the stairway. She moved the glasses and saw that Guardian was walking forward from the perimeter of the landing area towards the ship. He had reached the bottom of the stair by the time Captain Tryon's foot touched the surface of Isis; and Olwen saw him hold out his hand in greeting to the newcomer. There was a moment's hesitation on the part of the Captain. Olwen saw it distinctly, even at this distance. Then the Captain's hand came out . . . reluctantly? . . . and the two men formally shook hands.

It is I who should be down there welcoming the Captain, thought Olwen crossly. Now that the unthinkable impossible event had actually taken place she was devoured with curiosity. What were the two of them talking about, down there under the squat shadow of Pegasus Two? It simply wasn't fair of Guardian to have excluded her from this first historic meeting. After all, she told herself, I am the Keeper of the Isis Light, not Guardian. She nearly fell over the edge, leaning eagerly forward, as if an extra centimetre closer would enable her to hear what the two of them were saying.

They parted, not with a handshake this time. Guardian bowed slightly, in a subservient way that Olwen had never seen him use before, and which she found unexpectedly irritating. The Captain once more climbed the stairway back into his ship. It was not until he had vanished into the shadow of the open doorway that Guardian himself turned and left, to walk across the flame-scarred circle to where he had left the floater car parked safely among the long grasses.

So it is over. They are here, thought Olwen. She stood up and stretched and stowed the binoculars away in their case. Isis looked as it had always looked. The rolling ridges of mountain, rose-red and purple-streaked, their lower slopes

17

silvered over with thorn bush and cactus, stretched away to the horizon. If she stepped back two metres from the edge, so that Pegasus Two and the scorched circle of earth around it were blocked by the edge of the mesa, it was almost as if today had not happened. As if Isis was as it had always been. She sighed, remembering her birthday wish. Only in real life a thing did not cease to exist just because she, Olwen, could no longer see it.

By the time she had scrambled down the stone ladder to the house Guardian was just parking the floater at the end of the terrace. He looked as imperturbable as ever—as if greeting settler ships from five parsecs away was something that happened every day.

"Well?" she gasped, out of breath from her hasty descent.

"Well what?"

"Did you ask him to come to dinner? The *Captain*. Honestly, Guardian, don't tell me that you actually forgot to ask him to dinner?"

"You know I forget nothing. The moment was not propitious, that was all. I sent him your greetings in the proper fashion. I explained to him that your meeting with him and the passengers should wait upon a clean bill of health from the ship's doctor."

"Guardian, if they didn't get ill in space, why should they be ill now? And why should I catch anything anyway? I never do. You fuss entirely too much."

"Perhaps. But the fact remains that you have been exposed to no microbes for . . . for many years. We must take reasonable precautions."

"*You* didn't take precautions, did you?"

"Well, me . . . I've told you many times that I'm immune from all human flaws and failings."

Olwen laughed. "Making jokes is all very well, Guardian, but what I want to know is, when *do* I get to meet Captain Jonas Tryon?"

"Is it so important to you, Olwen?" Guardian sounded almost sad. "Have you been lonely all this time. I thought . . ."

"Oh, no! You know it isn't that. I'm just so curious. Another *person*. I wonder what we'll talk about . . .

18

what he'll think of Isis. Of me. Suppose they don't like me? Oh, Guardian!"

"Of course they'll like you. Why should they not? And you will get to meet the Captain and the settlers quite soon. I am planning to make you a costume—a sort of protective suit. And you must promise never to go down into the valley without it."

"You make it sound as if the Earth people were . . . well, as if they were diseased or something. Dangerous."

"To you they might be. Bear with me, my dear, and give me your word that you will not go down into the valley until I have made the suit for you."

"You're a fuss-pot, Guardian dear. But I love you. You have my word. Only please hurry and make the suit as soon as you possibly can."

The rest of that day Olwen spent on the mesa top, watching the settlers unload their ship and set up an instant village on the eastern shore of the lake. It was a good place, she had to admit, if one had to choose to live in the bottom of a valley where the air was as thick as treacle. The eastern mountains rose almost sheer behind the site, and curved around to the north, protecting the spot to some extent from the force of the equinoctial gales. Across the lake from the village was a grove of trees, with a sweet bready fruit in season; and the lake itself was bursting with fish and crustaceans, all of them good to eat. If they took care to keep the water clean, the river, flowing down from the Cascades and into the lake at its northern end, would supply good drinking water for ever.

The settlers had brought small tracked vehicles with them, similar to the one Guardian used for survey work when he didn't want to use a floater; and every man, woman and child from the ship strained and heaved to pile the vehicles high with plastic containers full of goods. Trip after trip they made, around the south end of the lake, over a bridge which they had laid down across Lost Creek, and so around to the new village. Before long there was a trampled track through the long plumed grass, and muddy scars at the verges of Lost Creek. Within a few hours houses began to appear. They were light plastic shells that were sprayed with stuff from a wheel-mounted tank to form a thick skin. From the top of the mesa they looked like the fat cocoons of the cactus moth.

Slowly, inexorably, the face of the plain was being changed. Ever since Isis had vegetation, ever since the mountains had been formed, this valley had lain there, grass-filled and still except for the tiny movements of deer and nesting birds. And now it would never be the same again. Never.

I hate it, Olwen thought passionately. I wish they had never come. She turned her back on the southern end of the mesa top and looked out across the rest of her kingdom. It was all right. It was as perfect as it had always been . . . But it wasn't the same any more. In spite of herself she found herself drawn back to the edge of the southern cliff. She sat with her back against a sun-warmed stone, her knees hugged to her chest, and watched the intense orderly activity down in the valley. Now and then a voice, louder than the others, carried up to her clifftop viewpoint. And there was laughter.

Laughter! Guardian never laughed. Odd, she had never thought about that before. He never laughed. She put her head on her knees. There was a funny feeling inside her, an empty wrenching sort of ache. It was a bit like the way she felt at the song of the upland lark. She suddenly felt that she wanted to cry. Cry? She had not cried in years . . . why should she? Guardian was perfect. He gave her everything she needed and everything she wanted that was good for her to have. Why should she want to cry as if she had lost something important? . . . No, as if she had found out that she had once lost something, long ago, something she couldn't remember?

Hobbit came bounding up the precipitous side of the mesa, his huge claws striking sparks off the rocks. He was wildly excited at the activity in the valley below, and he was panting, his many-toothed mouth open, his metre-long tongue lolling. He, like herself, was a creature of the uplands, and, like her, found what was going on in the valley below profoundly disturbing. Olwen put her arms around him, and buried her head in his hairy side. She could hear the regular bump-rumble of his double heart. It was comforting, and she clung to him until the long shadows and the chill in the air reminded her that Ra had dropped below the western mountains and that it was more than time to go home for supper.

20

Two days later Guardian had her germ-free suit ready. As with everything he made for her, it was a perfect fit, a silver jumpsuit with boots and finger-fitting gloves all in one, and pressure-seal zippers to make it easy to get off and on. The head covering was a surprise to Olwen. "Why not a helmet with a transparent face-plate, like a space suit?" she asked.

"Isn't this nicer?" He sounded oddly evasive and she frowned. But she had to admit that the new face-piece was very attractive. Guardian had modelled it with human features, of an opaque tinted plastic. The eyes were crystalline, and the nostrils were covered with a special permeable plastic. "If the air comes in, surely germs can too?" she objected. "And how am I supposed to eat? Or talk, come to that?"

"I promise you that you will not be exposed to germs. The membrane will do a perfect job of filtering the air. As for eating, it would not be advisable for you to eat the settlers' food, until they become aclimatized and start living off Isis. As for talking, did anything ever stop you? Of course you'll be able to talk."

"Without moving my lips? Mumble, mumble."

"Why don't you try it and see? Then you can tell me if there really is anything wrong with it."

"All right then. But I'm not convinced. I still think the whole idea of germs is ridiculous. That's a funny looking face. Is it supposed to look like me?"

Guardian didn't answer, but held the suit out to Olwen in such a resigned and downtrodden way that Olwen got the giggles. She slipped out of her clothes and into the new suit. "It *is* comfortable. Can you hear me properly? I *feel* mumbly."

"Your voice is perfectly clear."

"How do I look with my new face? Oh, why don't we have a mirror here? Really, it's the stupidest thing."

"You have never asked for one before."

"I just wish I knew what I looked like right now. I wonder what they'll think of me. Do you think they'll like me? Suppose they don't? Oh, Guardian!" She sat down abruptly.

"What is it? Are you ill? Let me take your pulse."

21

She shook her head. Her hands went up to her face, felt the unexpectedness of smooth plastic and fell into her lap. "Oh, Guardian, I'm scared!"

"I assure you that there is nothing to be afraid of. The Captain, the crew, the settlers—they are all your friends. They are all anxious to meet you. After all, you are something of a celebrity—the youngest Keeper of the Light in the galaxy! And I will be beside you all the time."

"You will? Oh, that's good. I thought . . . Are we going now?"

"Goodness, no. Captain Tryon is expecting us at eleven hours."

"Captain Jonas Tryon. Isn't it a magnificent name, Guardian? Oh, how am I going to remember their names and faces? Suppose they all look alike, what will I do?"

"They won't. And you have an excellent memory and accurate perceptive abilities. After all, you can tell Hobbit apart from any other hairy dragon, can't you? And you've given names to all the dormice families on the mesa top. Many people would find it difficult to distinguish between one dormouse and another. I find it quite a challenge myself. I promise you, people are easier. You have nothing to worry about."

Olwen took a deep breath. She smoothed the plastic of her silver suit over her knees. "You're quite right. What a comfort you are, Guardian dear. And the suit *is* comfortable. Only . . . how nice it will be when we've all got used to each other, and I can give a dinner party out there on the terrace, and wear my beautiful musical dress instead of this. Will it be very long?"

"Not long," he replied, but in a tone of voice that Olwen recognised as evasive. She frowned and sighed and went away to take off the suit.

Promptly at eleven, after the noon meal, at which Olwen ate very little, she and Guardian took the floater down from the terrace, hovering over the Cascades before spinning downriver to land in the very centre of the new village.

There were now eight of the "instant" houses, all positioned on flat ground well above the lake. The foam she had seen being pumped over the shells had dried to a creamy

22

rock-hard finish. The houses had been fitted with strong doors and with plastic windows, and, though they lacked the spaciousness of her own home, they looked comfortable enough.

Guardian parked the floater in front of the central building, above which the flag of Earth Government now flew in the brisk northwest wind. When he had climbed out he walked quickly around the floater and solemnly offered his arm to Olwen. Suppressing a giggle that threatened to bubble up in her throat, she climbed out with dignity, instead of vaulting over the side as she would ordinarily have done.

An enormous crowd had gathered in the central square in front of the main building. It was almost a relief to recognise among the sea of strange faces the tanned and rugged features of the Captain of the Pegasus. Her hand tightened on Guardian's arm, and he squeezed her hand encouragingly before leading her forward. He bowed slightly, and in a voice more rigidly formal than usual said, "Olwen, may I present Captain Jonas Tryon of the STC ship Pegasus Two. Captain, it is my honour to introduce Olwen Pendennis, the Keeper of the Isis Light."

Chapter Three

The warning klaxons awakened the sleeping passengers of the Interstellar Ship Pegasus Two. For the duration of the five-parsec journey from Earth all eighty of them had lain cocooned in an hypnotically induced slumber, while information about their new life on Isis was fed to them. Meanwhile, as they floated against their padded couch straps, dreaming and learning, the Captain and crew of the Pegasus had kept the ship on course from reference light to reference light, homing in to three-dimensional space, checking their coordinates, and winking out into hyper-space to the next light. To some super observer in space their progress across the galazy from Earth to Ra in the constellation Indus must have looked like an enormously long dotted line, as they alternately vanished and reappeared, arcing imperceptibly towards the centre of the slowly spinning galaxy.

The first thing Mark London was aware of was the apparent weightlessness of his body against the contoured couch on which he had spent the last months. In actual fact, the gravitational field of Ra was already making itself felt. The stylo that the navigational officer had left in mid-air almost a moment before had just reached the table top. But compared to Mark's last memory, lying apprehensively waiting for blast-off from Earth, he was weightless. It was a pleasant feeling, half awake, half asleep, wholly contented.

The quiet voice that had been his sole companion through the voyage spoke again in his ear. "You have had an excellent sleep. You have awakened fit and refreshed, remembering everything you have learned. Lie still until the nurse reaches you to detach your intravenous feeder. Then sit up very slowly, swing your legs down off the couch, and do the prescribed exercises."

Mark lay staring up at the white bulkhead until a twinge in his left arm and the firm pressure of an adhesive bandage triggered his next reaction. Obediently he sat up and swung his stiff legs down from the couch. His toes prickled with pins and needles, but otherwise he felt in perfect shape. He wriggled his toes and rotated his ankles, breathing deeply to the bottom of his lungs. He coughed. His throat and lungs felt dry and unused. So did his mouth. A drink would be good.

In the next beds his mother, father and little sister Carrie all seemed safe and well. The nurse was helping Carrie to sit up. Well, that was all right then . . . not that things often went wrong in space-flight. Hypno-sleep cushioned the body and mind against the insults of g-forces and weightlessness as the ship popped in and out of real space, and from the boredom of the time between . . . but it was good to see his family safe, with his own eyes.

Six hours later the passengers had had two meals and a full physical workout. By then Ra's gravitational pull was noticeable. An object put down, stayed down. An object forgetfully left in mid-air fell to the floor with a crash. Not that the settlers made that particular mistake. It was the crew, every time, who forgot. It was not surprising. Mark saw, in the occasional glimpse of a lined face, the strain of re-entry after months of weightlessness.

Every moment not spent in eating was spent in restoring the tone to flaccid muscles. Twenty-four hours after waking, Mark felt that he had never been in such good shape in his life before. Reluctantly he returned to his couch to strap himself in for planet-fall. His heart began to pound so hard with excitement that Mark was afraid it would show up on the bio-monitor, and he forced himself to practise the slow deep breathing that was one of the skills he had learned in hypno-sleep.

A final blast of the klaxon. Probably a warning for the crew to strap themselves in for planet-fall. "Planet-fall". The old sea term "land-fall" had been carried over into space navigation and now had more meaning than it had ever had back on Earth. Planet-fall . . . a fall towards a planet. Controlled by retro-jets, but nevertheless a fall, as the gravity of

Ra's fourth planet Isis reached out and grabbed them.

Outside Pegasus Two the heat shields began to glow and flake away in a spume of bright sparks. The atmosphere here was deeper than Earth's but thinner. Less friction, then, but for a longer period of time. Hot enough. Mark felt the perspiration trickle down the sides of his forehead and neck to be absorbed damply into the cushion against which his head was pressed. Experimentally he tried to move his right hand against the straps. Then just the tip of his index finger. As the ship hurtled towards Isis the reactionary forces pushed him with a giant's hand back against his couch. Breathing was almost impossible. It was something you did through your clenched teeth, drawing in a few cubic centimetres of air at a time, as much as you could force in, which was just enough to stop your eyes from bursting out of your head. The tearing thundering noises that surrounded him seemed to be an echo of what was going on inside his own body.

Mark was just beginning to realise, in a rising wave of panic, that he simply could not last another minute, when the noise stopped abruptly. The giant's hand was lifted from his body. He cautiously drew in a deep breath. Then another. Boy, that felt good!

The silence was overwhelming. Had he gone deaf? Then, as the pounding in his ears subsided and his heart slowed to its normal steady beat, he began to hear the tiny pings and snaps of cooling metal. Then Carrie's voice . . . "Mummy?" And Jody's fretful wail from further down the ship. People stirred and sighed. Far away Mark could hear the sound of metal grating against metal.

Then, quite suddenly, the tired smelly recycled air was gone. Instead there was chill, a smell of dry grass, the lively scent of a herb, something like sage, but different, new. The tang of upland air. When Mark sucked in the air he could feel it tingling right down to his toes. They had arrived! How much longer were they supposed to go on lying here? They were on Isis at last. Would the word to go ashore never be given? All around were the little sounds of breathing and fidgeting. All eighty settlers waited for the word.

When it finally came training held firm. They sat up. The velcro straps were undone for the last time, and in an orderly fashion they lined up in the long passenger cabin and marched, two by two, down a spiral flight of stairs to the main exit of the ship. There was a flash of brightness that dazzled, but the outside stair was steep and Mark had to keep his eyes on the steps below him, while the next passenger crowded him from above. So his first glimpse of Isis was of nothing but the stubble of blue-grey grass and, all around the ship, black char from the jets.

But once he had lined up with his family and the rest of their Ten he had time to look around, past the hectares of grey grass bowing and nodding waist high in every direction, to the mountains that rose almost sheer on every side. Some of them were flat-topped, like the mesas of New Mexico and Colorado, while the others were jagged, young-looking, unworn by time and weather, all of a startling rose-red colour streaked with sombre purple.

Mark turned around. To the north of the ship the mountains grudgingly parted, leaving a small ravine, in the misty depths of which he could see flashes of white—a waterfall, perhaps. Beyond the ravine were the distant peaks of yet more mountains, lavendered by the distance between.

There was no sound anywhere, except for the low voices of the settlers, and the sharp pings of still cooling metal. The sky was wide and empty, enormously empty, and of a clear shrill cool green. The sun . . . Mark glanced up and then quickly turned away . . . the sun was small, brilliant and white, and the shadows it cast were as hard-edged as if they had been cut out of blue-grey cardboard.

He was nudged and pushed back into place, so that by the time the Captain came down the stairway, the settlers were ranked in orderly fashion in their Tens. First there were the ten couples under twenty years of age, many of whom had probably married in haste to meet the immigration requirements. Next to them stood the ten childless couples whose ages ranged from twenty to thirty. No small children were allowed. Nothing was known about the disorienting effect of the long sleep on small children, and anyway, it had been unanimously agreed by STC officials that small children were too much of a hazard and a source of heartbreak on new planets. They had to be watched constantly, and they seemed

27

to have an uncanny habit of putting new and untested substances into their mouths without asking first, and of making pets of unknown and potentially dangerous animals. So there were no young ones among the Tens.

The two Tens, where Mark and Carrie stood, consisted of the ten married couples between the ages of thirty and forty, who had between them twenty children, from the age of Jody, who was nine going on ten, and had been squeaked through because his mother and father had unique new-planet training, and Mark, who was seventeen. There were two more males than females in this teenage population. The computer estimated that in the first two years of a new colony, an average of three out of forty men would lose their lives, while only one out of forty women might be expected to die. Assembling the groups for the Tens was a touchy exercise for psychologists and computers alike.

They had come aboard as strangers, these four Tens. They had never met back on overcrowded Earth, yet now they were bound to each other by powerful hypnotic suggestions into one big loyal family. As Mark stood to attention waiting for the Captain's formal words he let his eyes slide to left and right. He recognised every person, knew each name, each personality, the part that each was to play in establishing a home in this new world.

The Captain was the only unknown, and this made him seem larger than life. He stood sturdily on the bottom rung of the metal staircase, his piercing blue eyes surveying his living cargo. Mark looked up at the seamed, space-ruddied face, the eyes narrowed against the cold brilliance of the morning sun; just for a moment he wished that he too could be a crew member of a space ship. To ply one's endless way through space from Earth to star colony and back. That would be a sight more glamorous than farming!

But then he looked up, past the Captain, past the battered hulk of Pegasus Two, to the clear empty sky, and he smelled again the delicious spicy cold scent of aromatic herbs, and thought—glamour be damned. Isis is *home*.

The Captain spoke briefly, a formal inauguration of the new colony, a prayer, a welcome and a warning. He and his ship would stay, like a lifeboat, for one turn of Isis about its sun. Then they would leave, probably for ever. If things went wrong, if the colony somehow refused to "jell", then before the year's end they would all have to return to Earth, the opportunity to escape the crowding and the shortages gone for ever. If they survived the first year Pegasus Two would leave and the settlers would be on their own.

The Captain returned to the ship, and the hypnotic teaching took over. Without fuss, with incredible efficiency, the settlers dogged open the cargo doors and began to unload the packing cases containing the nucleus of their new life. They had two tread-tracked cars and two small floaters, all of them solar powered. These were pushed down the ramp by shoulder power and left in the sun to recharge while the rest of the cargo was unshipped.

An engineering team went ahead to build a bridge across the river that flowed out of the southern end of the lake. These decisions had all been made, long ago, on Earth. The river, which plunged down from the northern mountains in a series of spectacular waterfalls, emerged from the wide lake in a placid stream and meandered in a leisurely fashion between groves of bamboo and clumps of marsh grass until it, unexpectedly and unaccountably, lost itself in the ground two kilometres to the south. The Keeper of the Light had named it Lost Creek, and so it was called on the colony maps.

By the time all the packing cases had been piled around the squat base of Pegasus Two, the crawlers and floaters had acquired sufficient energy to be used; then began a continuous trek to and from the new town site on the far side of the lake. The temporary bridge, a roll of flexible plastic matting, had been unrolled and laid in place across the tussocky swamp that bordered Lost Creek. It had been pegged in place and its plastic "memory" had been frozen with a high-speed catalytic spray. Now it lay, as rigid as iron, as strong as concrete, as if it had always been there. Young bamboo plants, their tattered grey and mauve leaves shimmering in the wind, bordered it on either side. Only around the edges did it get a little muddy, as the crawlers, heavily laden, moved from ship to town site and back.

Mark, Willi, Angus and Kano were set to erecting the huts that would be home for the Tens. There was a hut each for

29

the childless Tens, and two huts for the Tens with families. In front, closer to the lake, with a clearing in front of it, there was a double-sized hut that would be dining room, meeting hall, kitchen and everything else for the new colony.

The huts were shells of fine plastic film, like bubble tents, each fastened securely by metal posts driven firmly into the soil. Inside, simple screens of the same film divided the area into rooms, one for each couple, a pair for each couple with children. As the boys finished erecting each hut a team of sprayers followed, pumping plastic foam over the shell, inside and out. The stuff set pudding-hard in a moment, and by the end of the day, acted on by the ultra-violet of Isis' sun Ra, it would be like concrete.

There was a scramble of women behind the sprayers, fastening in shelves, hooks, hangers, while the walls were still soft, and another team cut holes for doors and windows. As soon as everyone else was out of the way there came the youngsters, each carefully carrying piles of family possessions, blankets, clothes, books and tools.

By lunch, which they ate sprawled on the dry spiky grass overlooking the lake, there was already a semblance of order. Before Ra touched the rim of the western mountains a stranger would have imagined that the village had been there for months.

Supper was a celebration, a properly cooked meal of freeze-dried turkey meat, with dressing, cranberry sauce and vegetables, followed by pumpkin pie, all transported from Earth in frozen packets to mark the settlers' first Thanksgiving Dinner.

Next year, thought Mark, looking round the lamplit dining room, next year we'll be on our own. No food from Earth then. The Pegasus will have left. What will Thanksgiving Dinner be like next year? It was a solemn scary thought. When at last they left the dining room, all of them reluctant to break away from the "together" feeling, even though they could hardly keep their eyes open, Mark walked a little way away from the huts and looked up at the night sky.

Here, closer to the centre of the galaxy, the stars burned twice as thickly as even in a southern sky back on Earth. The patterns of the constellations were new. Nothing was familiar

30

any more. He looked for Earth, but how could he tell, in that crowded sky? He knew that Sol was an insignificant star low down on the western horizon, in a constellation whose only interest was that its appearance would tell them that summer was on its way.

In the brilliant starshine he could just see the squat silhouette of Pegasus Two, a black outline against the dark expanse of grassland that spread from the far shore of the lake to the distant western mountains. He looked around. Above the eastern horizon a moon rose, tiny, hardly more than star size. It shunted busily among the thickly clustered stars, more like an artificial satellite than a real moon. That must be Shu. And somewhere up there, hidden like a tree in the middle of the forest, was Isis' second moon Nut. It was even tinier, and since it was in a wider orbit and moved more slowly, it would be even more unnoticeable.

For a second Mark felt a twinge, almost like stomach ache, for the familiar things of Earth, for a sun and moon that looked like the Sun and the Moon, for stars whose patterns were familiar. But then he remembered the actualities of the city where he and Carrie and their parents had lived; the choking smog, the hours standing on the rapid transit, shoulder to shoulder with other half-asleep commuters, the line-ups for food, for movies, for a day in the country or by the sea . . . the continual inhuman jostling for space.

Here on Isis there was at least space. A man could stretch and feel free to be himself. He took a last look around. The thin air was biting cold. To his right the mesa rose stark and steep, bisecting the sky, blotting out half the stars. Over to the north, near where he had seen the waterfall, halfway up the precipitous cliff, was light. Tiny golden oblongs of light that said clearly that up there, halfway to the sky, was a house. One of the lights blinked out, just for an instant, as if someone had walked across the room close to the window.

Mark realised with a shock that he must be looking at the dwelling of the Keeper of the Isis Light. That was strange and mysterious . . . a girl, all alone out here, parsecs from the nearest civilization, with no one to talk to but . . . what did she call him? . . . Guardian, that was it. Up there, where she lived, close to the mesa top, the stars must seem close enough

31

to touch, the burning cold of space must be a neighbour.

What would it be like to be alone for year after year, with only the night and the wind and the cold spicy smell of the upland grasses? He tried to imagine how she must feel—the Keeper of the Light—but try as he might his mind couldn't make the jump. His training told him too clearly that the uplands were dangerous, that he must never leave the valley without the protection of an ultra-violet-opaque suit and an oxygen mask.

One day, off in the vague future, if all went well with the colony, they would plant trees and gradually build up the oxygen content of Isis. Then the ozone layer would also thicken, the ultra-violet would be safely filtered out, and the mesas and mountains of Isis would be theirs . . . One day, but not now. For now, the valley was wide and deep. That was where they belonged, not in some oxygen-thin eagle's eyrie, perched on a cliff halfway to outer space.

He turned his back on the night and went into his own hut, into the room he shared with Carrie. She was already asleep, so he skinned quietly out of his clothes and slid into his sleeping bag. It was unbelievably quiet. There was no roar of cars, no tearing sound of jets, no warring voices from a thousand transistors, no quarrelling shouts, no kids screaming in the night, no sirens.

A tiny rustle in the stiff grass outside sent a shock of goose-flesh down his back. Far off there was the lonely yammering cry of some unknown night creature. He wriggled deeper into the warmth of his sleeping bag and found himself thinking again about the high mesa, and about the girl who had kept the light burning on Isis all the long years until they had come.

Chapter Four

Olwen found the initial meeting painfully awkward. She was accustomed to her relationship with Guardian. If he spoke, it was to her and to no one else, since there *was* no one else. When she spoke to him he would answer her directly, accurately, truthfully and to the point. Face to face with twenty people, all about her own age, backed up by a horde of elders, too many even to count, she was completely tongue-tied.

Even before they began to talk she could feel the curiosity, like eager fingers reaching out to touch and pinch. And when they did begin to talk it was all at once. They interrupted each other, they giggled and nudged. She wasn't even sure if they were talking to her or to each other.

Olwen felt her eyes sting and the corners of her mouth turn down, and she was thankful for the mask that hid her expression from them. Without it she would be completely vulnerable. With it she was still Olwen Pendennis, the Keeper of the Isis Light. She drew a shaky breath and suddenly remembered the words of greeting that she had planned.

"I would like to welcome you all to Isis," she spoke clearly over the whispers and giggles. "I hope you will be very happy here. When you have settled in and become acclimatized I would like to show you over my home, and the way up to the top of the mesa, and the trail to the northern mountains." She found that her shyness dropped from her as she spoke. After all, they were people, just as she was. They weren't going to eat her. "It's so beautiful up on top of Isis," she went on eagerly. "There are a million things to do, and I'll . . . well, I mean, I'll enjoy sharing them with you."

33

She had planned her welcoming speech with care, but it wasn't until she had spoken the words that she realised how true they were. She *was* looking forward to having friends, to showing off her beautiful Isis. She smiled behind her mask, and waited for them to respond, but all they did was to look at each other and shrug. Then two of them began to talk at once, got a fit of nervous giggles and subsided. A tall girl with a determined chin stepped forward. "Thanks. It's nice of you to offer, but the valley's our home. Up there . . . well, there's not enough air and the ultra-violet can kill you if you're not suited up, so what's the attraction? So, no thanks!"

The others nodded silent agreement, and Olwen felt her face growing hot under the mask. Didn't they want her friendship after all? She stuck her chin up. "I hope you enjoy your valley," she said coldly. "If you ever need me you know where I live."

She had turned her back on them and was walking rapidly away from the village when a voice called her name. It wasn't Guardian or the Captain or any of the grown-ups. Just one of *them*. She ignored the voice and walked even faster up-river, towards the Cascades. Guardian could take the floater home. All she wanted was to be alone.

What was the matter with her? She had been so angry when Guardian had first told her of the invasion of her Isis by these unknowns from Earth. Then, little by little, almost without being aware of it, she had begun to look forward to their arrival. She had day-dreamed about walking the mountains, sunning on the mesa top, scrambling up the Cascades, with a companion more responsive than Hobbit.

How stupid! It had never crossed her mind that they might totally reject her beautiful world of upper Isis, and with it, her. She sniffed back her tears and walked even faster, ignoring the voice behind her.

She was almost at the bottom of the Cascades when he caught up with her. "Do wait," he panted, and when she didn't stop he grabbed her hand. Even through the plastic of her suit she could feel its warmth. "Where are you off to in such a hurry?" he went on in the friendliest manner.

"Back home. Nobody needs me down here."

34

"But . . . the mesa top . . . exploring . . . didn't you mean what you said?"

"You *want* to go up there? But the others . . . they said . . . I thought . . ." Her voice died away as she looked up at him and saw him properly for the first time, not as one of a cluster of twenty Earth kids. He was as tall as Guardian, maybe taller. It was hard to be sure, because he was so slim, and the mop of brown hair, still unshorn after months of space-sleep, made him look even taller. His skin was funny, pale with pink cheeks and little brown dots, like a miniature milky way, across his nose and cheekbones. It looked so different from Guardian's smooth golden skin. The eyes were different too. They were blue streaked with brown. As she stared up at him the pupils contracted as the bright afternoon light of Ra teased his eyes. He shaded them with his hand, and, fascinated, she watched the pupils dilate and darken again.

"What on earth are you staring at? You'd think you'd never seen people before . . ." He stopped and then began to laugh, and she found herself joining in.

"You forgot—you're not on Earth any more. And of course I haven't, except for Guardian and Hobbit."

"Who's Hobbit? I thought you were alone here."

"He's my dearest friend, next to Guardian, of course. Guardian found him for me when he was just a pup."

"A *pup*? Oh, I see. Hobbit's a dog."

"Not really. But a bit like, only I think larger."

"I'd like to see him some time. Is he around?"

"He lives up in the high places. Up on the mesa. Or among the rocks at the top of the Cascades. He's shy."

"Like you?"

"Yes." She said it without meaning to. The word dropped like a stone into a sudden silence. She could feel the ripples from it going out in circles until they touched him. Until they surrounded them both. Her heart had started to pound uncomfortably, and she was finding it increasingly difficult to breathe. Bother this suit, she thought wildly. I'll have to get Guardian to make some adjustments or I'll suffocate.

His voice broke into her thoughts. It was a nice voice, not as incisive as Guardian's, but with a light warm feel to it, like

35

sunshine on the rocks, as if laughter was always just under the surface. ". . . I know your name," he was saying. "But you don't know mine. I'm Mark London. I'm here with my young sister Carrie and my parents. He's an agrarian specialist and she's a microbiologist."

The words drifted over Olwen's head. Young sister. Parents. "What's it like to have a real family?" she asked.

He hesitated. She felt that he was just about to say something and then was stopped by something inside himself. He shrugged. "Not much different from you and Guardian and Hobbit, I suppose. Any more questions?"

"Yes. What are those funny little brown specks all over your face? Do they grow there?"

He began to laugh in earnest. She saw that he had lovely white teeth, evenly spaced and strong. His laughter made her feel warm and pleased inside herself, and under the mask she smiled in response. "They're called freckles," he told her. "I hope you don't mind the look of them, because under this sun they'll be popping out like mushrooms after rain. Don't you have any under that mask of yours? It'd be a miracle if you didn't, living your whole life under this sun, up on the heights too."

"I don't think I have any. Are they bumpy? Let me feel." Before he could move she had run her fingertips over his cheeks and nose.

"Hey, that tickles! What's the matter? Why don't you look at your own face? You sound as if you never have."

"No, I suppose I haven't. Oh, I've seen myself in a pool, when the water's still, you know. And in a spoon, but I know I don't look like that. All fat and upside down."

"Don't you have any mirrors in that cave-house of yours?"

"Mirrors? No. It's funny, but we don't." She frowned.

"Oh, maybe your Guardian doesn't want you to get too vain," he teased, and when Olwen realised it was a joke she smiled back. He put out his hand in turn and touched her cheek. "I wish I could see you without that mask. Can't you take it off? What's it there for anyway?"

"No. Don't." She backed away from his touch. "Guardian says I must wear it every time I'm with you. You see, you might be carrying germs that I've never been exposed to . . ." Her voice trailed off. It sounded so rude, as if she thought they were dirty. Perhaps he'd be offended and go away. But it was all right.

He nodded quite understandingly. "Don't worry about it. I just hope you won't have to hide from us for too long, that's all. Though I think I can guess what you look like from your voice. It's an awfully pretty voice. Did any one ever tell you? . . . No, I don't suppose they did. And your height and shape and so on look just right . . ." He broke off, and she saw the pink in his cheeks suddenly deepen and run up into his forehead. She watched, fascinated, and wondered if her own colouring was as changeable. It was funny, but interesting. He coloured even more under her stare.

"I should be getting back," he said awkwardly. "There's still an awful lot of work to do. But did you mean it? About taking us up to the top of the mesa and into the mountains?"

"I thought you didn't want to go."

"I can't answer for the others. But I certainly do. As soon as we landed and I saw those mountains . . . Oh, I know it'll be difficult. We'll have to have oxygen and ultra-violet-opaque suits. But even so, I just have the feeling that it must be terrific up there. Would you take me some time when you're free?"

"Of course I will. And it is terrific. This valley isn't Isis at all. Isis is the mountains. I'll take you whenever you want."

"Tomorrow? Mid-afternoon? Will that be all right? I'll be working from sun-up till then."

"I'll meet you here at the bottom of the Cascades. Would eleven hours be too early?"

"Better make it twelve. I *think* that's right. In spite of hypnotic training I haven't really got used to the idea of a twenty hour day yet."

She laughed. "What other length could a day possibly be?"

"Would you believe twenty-four?"

"Sounds awfully clumsy."

"Whatever you're used to, I suppose. I'll see you tomorrow then."

"Yes. Of course. Tomorrow."

Suddenly enormously happy, Olwen watched Mark scramble down the rocks and across the river, at the place where it churned among the pebbles, getting rid of all its energy in a sudden flurry of white foam. She watched him until he was just a small figure trotting through the stubbly grass towards the village. Till he disappeared behind a hut. Till she could not see him any more.

She turned to scramble up the cliff to the house. She felt that she had never been able to move so fast. Her eyes had never been so keen, her hands so sure and strong, her feet so nimble. She was absolutely bursting with happiness.

The floater was parked at the end of the terrace. And she hadn't even noticed it go by! "Guardian!" She burst into the house. "Guardian, where are you"

"In the kitchen."

Olwen danced across the living room to the kitchen and put her arms around his waist and hugged him. "Oh, Guardian, guess what? I've found a friend."

"I am very glad for you, my dear."

"I never knew that having a friend would make one so happy, so *alive*. Do you know what I mean?"

"You always were completely alive."

"Not like this."

"No. You are right. Not like this. You *are* different." He turned from chopping vegetables to look at her, his expression unfathomable.

Olwen began to strip off her mask and suit. "Phoo! I'm glad I don't have to live in this thing."

"You were too warm?"

"Too . . . something. I'm not sure."

"As soon as you are sure I will adjust it for you. Meanwhile lunch will be ready in five minutes, if you would like to change and wash."

"Yes, I will. In a minute. Guardian, why haven't you made any mirrors for this house? It's so odd. I never thought about it till the other day. And just now. Mark asked me if I had freckles—that's what they're called—little brown sunspots all over the face—and I didn't even know if I had them. I felt really stupid, not knowing. Why don't we have any mirrors?"

"You never asked for one before the other day. What has changed?'

"I . . . I'm not quite sure." Olwen untied the mass of dark reddish brown hair that had been confined in her protective suit and shook it free so that it swirled around her shoulders. She picked up a strand and held it out in front of her. "Is it beautiful, Guardian? Is the colour beautiful?"

"Yes, it is."

"And the rest of me, that I can't see?"

"*I* think so."

"I wonder if Mark will. I wish I had a mirror. Guardian, will you please make one for me. A big one, so that I can see all of myself at once."

Guardian had turned to stir something on the stove. He said over his shoulder, "A mirror can only show you what *you* see as yourself. It cannot tell you what another person sees."

"Oh. What can?"

"Why, the other person."

Olwen sighed impatiently. "All Mark can see of me is that silly mask. And that's not me at all. Guardian, *must* I go on wearing it? Tomorrow I'm taking him to the top of the mesa, to show him *my* Isis. Must I wear my suit and mask then? There can't possibly be any germs up there. The wind will blow them right off the mesa and Ra will kill them."

Guardian shook his head, but she went on eagerly. "Don't forget, Mark will be wearing a UVO suit and breathing mask. How can he possibly spread germs through that?"

"You have a most logical mind, Olwen." Guardian's even voice sounded to her keen ear a little troubled. "And your conclusions are substantially correct. Nevertheless, I will ask you to wear the suit and mask whenever you are going to meet any of the new settlers, no matter where, or how they are dressed."

"But why? Why *should* I?"

"Because I ask you to. For your own good. No other reason."

"OHHH!" Olwen screamed in exasperation, and then laughed. "Do you realise that you're actually being illogical, Guardian? But . . . all right. I'll do as you ask. Only the

39

mesa won't be the same without the feel of the wind and the heat of Ra on my skin."

"The material of your suit is very thin. I think you will be comfortable."

"You're a dear, Guardian, even when you're being exasperating, and I do understand you're only thinking of me. Only . . . oh, well, I suppose I'll still be better off than Mark in his UVO suit and oxygen equipment."

After lunch the next day Olwen climbed down from the house to the bottom of the Cascades, and sat on a wide slab of orange rock covered with blue-grey lichen, which turned to a vivid blue where it was soaked by the spray of the waterfall. It was almost twelve hours. And the day had never gone so slowly.

She looked down the long valley towards the village on the east bank of the lake. There were tens of little black figures swarming around like fire-ants, but none of them was recognisably Mark. What could he be doing that was so important that he couldn't be on time? What would he be doing anyway? She knew nothing about what he did, nothing about his life. Nothing except for the fact that he was . . . Mark.

She lay back on the rock and stared up at the face of the mesa that seemed to plunge dizzily away from her to the sky. Soon she would be up there, on top of Isis, where the winds swept cold and clean. Nothing moved among the rocks. Where was Hobbit? she wondered idly, and realised guiltily that she hadn't spared him a thought since the landing of Pegasus Two. Should she call to him now and introduce him to Mark? But then he was so friendly that he was almost impossible to get rid of, once she had wakened him from his afternoon sleep. Just for this once she wanted Mark to herself. All to herself.

A pebble spun and dropped into the water with a plop and she sat up suddenly. He was there, looking even taller than before as he stood above her. Her heart gave an unexpected painful bound.

"I'm sorry I'm a bit late. I had to finish what I was on."

"You're not late. I just got here myself," she lied happily.

He had a fascinatingly bony face, she thought, with a nose that jutted determinedly out from his forehead, and a smile that made her feel warm clear through. She still sat on the rock, staring up at him. "I don't even know what you do," she said slowly, at last. "I know nothing about you, nothing at all."

He dropped to his knees beside her. "We've got lots of time," he said comfortably. She glowed inside. That meant, didn't it, that they were going to go on being friends? For ever.

When Olwen didn't answer Mark looked around, taking in the triple waterfall, the jewel colours of the wet rocks, and the dizzy height of the mesa above them.

"Wow! It's tremendously steep. It looks much worse close to. I wonder if I'll be able to make it. I'm no mountain climber."

"Of course you will. There's nothing to it. Guardian even lasered out steps in the difficult places. Don't worry. I'll show you. If you put your hands and feet exactly where I do it'll be easy. What about your equipment?"

"All here." He showed her the small tank slung over his shoulders, and strapped on a face-mask with a heavily tinted eye-piece, which Olwen supposed he must need to protect his eyes from Ra's powerful light.

"Are you all ready? Then follow me, and remember, watch where I put my hands and feet." Olwen ran nimbly across the stone-littered slope to the base of the mesa, and began to climb the path that led from the Cascades up to the house. She took her time and was not even breathing deeply when she reached the terrace. She looked back to see Mark labouring up the slope behind her. She held out a firm hand and hauled him bodily the last couple of metres up to the terrace. He sucked desperately at his oxygen supply and dropped into the nearest chair. After a few minutes he was able to wheeze painfully, "Sorry. Out of practice."

Olwen, who had begun to feel rather smug, guiltily realised that Mark's only preparation for the climb had been the three days of working around the village, after months of space-sleep. "I *am* sorry. I forgot. We can stay here as long as you like, go up to the top another day, if you'd rather."

41

Mark pulled off his mask, and held it in one hand, so that he could breathe comfortably into it and talk at the same time. His lips were awfully blue, she noticed, and wondered if she should call Guardian. "Perhaps I'd better acclimatize. This is pretty high for me anyway. What a view though! Why, back home, people would pay a fortune to stay in a hotel with a view like this."

"It is marvellous, isn't it? Guardian picked the spot, and hollowed the rooms right out of the solid rock. He decorated the rooms and made all the furniture too."

"He sounds pretty perfect—this Guardian of yours."

"Oh, he is. He's wonderful. He designed my new bedroom and he makes all my clothes. Just wait until I can show you the dress he gave me for my birthday! He . . ."

"Hey." Mark leaned forward and touched her hand. "I'm sure that he's all you say. But I'd rather talk about you than him."

"Oh." She stared. His eyes crinkled at the corners when he smiled. "There's nothing to know about me. I'm dull," she said uncertainly.

"Dull? You're crazy! All these years alone on a planet. What do you think about? What music do you like? Do you play anything yourself? Do you sing? What about poetry? History? Do you have any books?"

"Oh, I see." Olwen rearranged her thoughts. She and Guardian often talked about books and music. If she told him impulsively that she *loved* Mozart's Horn Concerti, then Guardian would analyse them, movement by movement, until she was aware of their perfection. It was interesting to know *why* she liked a particular piece; but she knew somehow, that Mark wasn't talking about likes and dislikes the way Guardian did. She took a deep breath.

"I like Bach and Beethoven, especially the symphonies . . . oh, and the Choral! Talking of choral, don't you think Handel is wonderful? We've got a lot of tapes of his oratorios. And I love the 1812 Overture. Do you know, it's exactly like a spring storm on Isis. I wonder how Tchaikowsky knew? And then . . .."

"Whoa!" Mark laughed. "That's not a conversation, that's a list. Go slowly. We've got lots of time."

42

There. He'd said it again. Lots of time. Time for talking. Time for friendship. So why did she have this scary feeling that every second with him was precious, and she must snatch it because it might be the last?

"I'm sorry," she said humbly. "I don't know how to have this kind of conversation. You'll have to show me. With Guardian it's different, and the rest of the time there's just been me, or me and Hobbit, which I suppose is much the same thing really."

"Unless Hobbit can talk. Can he?"

She laughed. "Silly. He's only an animal, even though he's my friend. I've often wished he *could* talk so that we could have proper conversations."

"Well, I'm here now, so you don't need a talking Hobbit. But you've got to give me a chance to listen to what you're saying, and to tell you what I think back. Do you see? Let's go back to Bach . . ."

Ra dropped slowly into the western sky and sank below the top of the mesa, so that its shadows subdued the silver waterfalls to pewter. Guardian came out onto the terrace to remind Olwen that he would be serving dinner in half an hour.

"I can't believe it. The whole afternoon has vanished!" Olwen exclaimed.

"And I still have to see the view of Isis from the top of the mesa."

"We've got lots of time," she quoted back at him, and laughed at the thought.

"You've got a pretty laugh. But I wish I could see your real smile, underneath the mask."

"Guardian, couldn't I take it off? Please? And aren't you going to ask Mark to stay for dinner?"

"Not this time, Olwen." Guardian's voice was firm. "And you must continue to wear your suit and mask whenever you are close to the settlers."

"We really don't have any germs, you know," Mark put in quietly. "We were all certified disease-free before leaving Earth."

"All humans have bacteria in their digestive tract. They are beneficial to you. They may not be so to Olwen."

43

"She's human too!"

"She has been separated from you all for so long."

Mark nodded and sighed. "He's right, Olwen. And you can't be too careful. Anyway, I must go. Our supper is at fifteen hours too and I'm going to be late. I'd hate to have a search party out after me. Will you take me up to the top of the mesa next time? I promise I'll be in better shape."

"Of course. When? Tomorrow?"

"Maybe the day after."

"Same time?"

"I'll try and be earlier. No, tell you what. Come down to the village as soon as you've had your noon meal. There's someone there I'd really like you to meet. I've got an idea." Mark got to his feet and adjusted his oxygen mask over his face.

"Shall I come with you? Can you manage? Or would you rather Guardian took you back in the floater. It'd be no trouble." But her suggestions seemed to offend him, Olwen couldn't see why, and she stood hesitantly, looking over the balustrade, while Mark scrambled and slid painfully down to the valley floor far below.

"Perhaps we should have better lighting down there, Guardian. It's hard to see some of the footholds in the dusk."

"You've never had any difficulty seeing your way."

"I think my eyes are better than his—I mean, than theirs."

"That is undoubtedly true. You are perfect in all particulars."

"Oh, Guardian, honestly! Don't say things like that when Mark—when other people—are around. I'd feel so stupid. I wonder if Mark thinks I'm perfect. Do you suppose maybe he does?"

"It is quite possible." Guardian turned abruptly and went back into the kitchen, leaving Olwen to lean against the stone balustrade, idly watching the last reflections of Ra on the far eastern mountains.

When Guardian came to the door to tell her that supper was ready she had not moved, though now she was looking down the valley, at the fire-fly lights of the new village. It was an unusually still night, and the lights were reflected in

44

the waters of the lake, as if the early stars had fallen and drowned.

Two days later, after an extra early lunch, Olwen climbed nimbly down the stone staircase and picked her way along the rocky riverbank. It was a perfect day for the mesa top, clear and cool and almost calm. Her eager footsteps slowed as she got closer to the cluster of houses. Where would she find Mark? How should she ask?

But it was all right. He must have been on the look-out for her. "How are you?" He took both her hands.

"I'm fine." She smiled back, and then remembered what he had said about conversations. "How are you?"

"We've been busy, I can tell you. But at least my muscles are in better shape now. I'll make it to the top of the mesa or die in the attempt."

"No!" She put her hand on his arm.

"Olwen, that was a joke!"

"Oh, I see. I guess I don't like jokes about dying. Are you ready to go?"

"Hold on. The mesa won't run away . . . that's another joke, by the way. But don't you remember? I wanted you to meet someone. Don't worry. He's very nice. He's our doctor, Phil MacDonald."

"Why do you want me to meet him? I don't need to meet anyone else now I've met you, do I?"

"Of course. You'll have to meet all of us eventually. After all, we're all going to share Isis for the rest of our lives. But there's a special reason why I want you to meet Phil now. You see, I've talked to him, and he disagrees with . . . with Guardian. He thinks that you have no need of any protective suit or mask. He thinks Guardian is being unnecessarily fussy. Now don't you want to come and talk to him?"

"Yes, of course. But I can't allow him to change my mind, Mark. You see, I made Guardian a solemn promise."

"I do understand. What I thought was, maybe we could get Phil to talk to Guardian and change his mind for him, maybe with some modern scientific proof."

"That would be wonderful. If he can", she added doubtfully.

"He's in the hospital. I'll introduce you, and then go and get into my gear."

Phil MacDonald was not much older than Mark, and not a bit frightening, Olwen discovered. "What I really would like to do," he explained when the introductions were over. "Is, with your permission, to take a sample of your blood. After a few days of tests I should be able to prove conclusively to Guardian that there is no danger in your mixing with any of the settlers."

"That would be wonderful." Olwen beamed and instantly stuck out her left arm.

"Through the sleeve of your suit? That won't be so easy. But I suppose it would be cheating if you slipped out of it even for a second."

"I promised, you see."

"All right. But I'd better get a thicker needle."

"My suit is really quite thin. A one-way permeable plastic, Guardian said."

"If you say so, little lady. Now hold still. Blast! Thin, you say? It's bent the needle! Now, let's try again. Yell if I hurt. Okay? You're sure? Got it." He withdrew the sample and slipped it into the refrigerator. "I must say your Guardian's idea of a thin membrane and mine don't coincide. It felt more like rhinoceros hide! Is your arm sore?"

Olwen laughed. "Not a bit. Thank you for taking the trouble. Will you let me know just as soon as you can. I want to take Mark on a picnic."

"Lucky Mark. In the interests of young love, then. As soon as possible, if not sooner."

Olwen blushed under her mask, and stood shyly wondering what to say next.

"Go on," the doctor urged her. "Scat! He'll be waiting for you by now, and I've got to get this hospital sorted, as well as removing cactus spines from a bunch of unwary teenagers!"

Chapter Five

Mark had never had to work his body so hard in his whole life as he did on the climb from the valley floor close to the Cascades up to the top of Lighthouse Mesa. This time they paused for only a second on the terrace of Olwen's house, halfway up the cliff. "Until you get your second wind," she had said briskly.

He had wanted to tell her, as they set out again, that he hadn't even found the rest of his first wind, much less got on to the second, but he had not enough spare breath to talk at all. When she started out he had to follow her. From the southern end of the terrace—how good the hammock looked, swinging gently in the shade of the rocky overhang—the track, that she called a staircase, wound upward, became invisible, reappeared again incredibly small and far away.

He swallowed a sudden gush of saliva that he knew was pure fear, and tried to make each breath come slowly and evenly. He knew, though it was hard to make his panting chest believe it, that too much oxygen could be as dangerous as too little. Either would make him dizzy, and if he got dizzy even for a second . . . He looked down, and then, gulping, very quickly looked up again, at the figure of Olwen above him.

She was unbelievably nimble, and as unafraid—no, as unaware of the horrifying height as a mountain goat. Her fingers and toes seemed to find cracks and slits in the rockface that he never saw at all until she pointed them out to him; and all the time she kept up a light flow of talk. Today he did not bother to teach her the art of give-and-take in conversation. He was only too thankful that she did not demand answers. He needed every cubic centimetre of air for the climb itself.

"This stretch used to be quite difficult," she said chattily, swarming up a totally sheer stretch of rock. "When I was very small Guardian used to bring me up here piggy-back. Then once my legs were long enough for the climb, he lasered out notches in the rock. Now it's practically a proper staircase."

In a pig's eye it is, thought Mark vulgarly, stretching his arm almost out of its socket for the next handhold. His UVO suit was a sweat bath, and the perspiration was beginning to fog his face-mask. Once he had to stop, inelegantly spread-eagled against the side of the cliff, until it cleared enough for him to see the next steps.

On his first days on Isis Mark had not been particularly aware of the weight difference. Isis was only a little more dense than Earth. But now, climbing, so it seemed, right up into the sky, the extra five kilos of body weight seemed to be hanging like lumps of lead from his arms and legs. But he climbed doggedly on, determined not to give in, determined to see the true Isis that Olwen talked about.

He stared at the streaked reddish purple rock a few centimetres from his face until his eyes began to water. He looked up only for the next handhold. On and on. Then, quite suddenly, Olwen was no longer there. A moment later there was a cool breeze on the little patch of skin between the front of his hood and the eyepiece of his face mask. There was a sensation of brightness above him. He forced his legs to push the rest of him up that last two metres, and then he rolled over onto a flat patch of grass.

He lay on his back, his eyes shut against the sudden glare, struggling to push the air in and out of his lungs.

"Are you all right?" She was leaning over him in an anxious mother-hen attitude.

He tried to smile nonchalantly, realised that she couldn't see through his breathing mask, and gave up the attempt. "Few minutes . . . give me . . . just a few minutes," he managed to force the words out past his heaving chest and pounding heart.

She nodded and walked casually away. After a time Mark began to feel that he wasn't going to die just then, and he sat up cautiously and looked around. He was facing north, so that his first view of upper Isis was of the great mountains rolling away to north and east and west in great red and purple breakers. He felt that he could see—or was he just imagining it?—the gentle curve of the planet.

The sky was of a deep intense blue-green, with no vestige of cloud, and his shadow ran sharp-edged and blue across the wide plateau in front of him. He could feel the breeze, but it was too gentle to move the strange antique shapes of cactus, grey and brown and silver, and it barely stirred the stubbly brittle grass.

A very long way off he saw a single dot in the empty sky. It grew larger, swooped, and became a bird, eagle-sized, which dropped suddenly and soared again, a small dun object dangling in its talons. He heard its triumphant scream, a tiny sound, sharper than the breeze, but barely any louder. A tiny far-off sound, the only sound in the world. He sat very still and listened to the silence . . .

When at last he got to his feet and turned around it was a shock to see the great dish antenna of the Lighthouse, and beyond it, dizzying depths below, the squat shape of Pegasus Two, standing alien, in an ugly circle of blackened stubble. The plumed grass had been trampled flat by feet and crawlers and more feet. Around the bridge across Lost Creek he could see from up here the blackish-red stains of mud where the ground had been chewed up by the tracks of the crawlers. It looked as if Isis itself had been wounded and had bled.

Olwen was sitting propped against the supports of the antenna, her arms circling her knees, staring into space. What must she think of their coming? Their invasion? He blurted out, "You must have hated it when we came, spoiling the newness."

She looked up at him quickly. The blank charm of her face mask told him nothing, but her voice was warm and surprised. "Oh, I did. Then afterwards I felt so guilty. After all, that is what the Keeper of the Light is for, to make a planet safe for other people to come to. But I couldn't see it that way at first. I hated you, all of you. Imagine you understanding that!"

He dropped to the ground beside her. "What must it have been like, having a whole planet to yourself?"

"I can't begin to tell you how wonderful it was. It was as if every day was a present. What was it like living on a planet crowded with people? I suppose you must have met, oh, a hundred people a day! It makes my head spin to think about."

"A hundred a day?" Mark's laugh was bitter. "You're thinking about villages in the outback, or in the middle ages. Listen. I'll tell you what it was really like, if you want to know."

"Go on."

"We lived in an apartment block that had four units. Each unit was thirty-five storeys high. Each floor had fifty apartments, with an average of four people in each . . . parents and two children, you know. Two children are the most a family is allowed, even with planning permission. So there were about twenty-eight thousand people in our apartment block alone. We lived in a suburban ring that surrounded the city. I don't know how many apartments like ours there were. Hundreds anyway. You could never be truly alone, not for a minute." His hands clenched at the thought. She put a gentle hand on his arm and he let out his breath in a sigh. "That's why we take the risk of colonizing, of course. A new planet. A new chance to begin again, instead of having to patch up all the old mistakes. The ship could be meteor-struck, or lost in between-space. It could crash or burn up on entry. The planet might turn out to be a nightmare in spite of all the computer care in choosing it. But it's still worth the risk. Anything is worth the risk, just to get away."

Olwen did not answer for a while. When she did her voice was soft and trembled, almost as if there were tears in it. "I feel so selfish, to have had this beauty and peace all to myself for ten years."

"Ten? I thought you were born here?"

"Yes. Oh, sixteen of your years."

"I was forgetting. Were you never lonely?" He looked past the valley to the far southern mountains and at the empty sky, and suddenly shivered. What could it have been like for a child, alone?

She shook her head. "Lonely? There has always been Guardian. Why should I be lonely?" He couldn't think of

50

anything to say, and after a minute she went on. "What about you? Does Isis seem very empty and frightening to you?"

"In a way. But we do have each other. Eighty people is a very small group to start anything big, like a new planet. It's the smallest group I have ever been with. But the hypno-teach made us feel close to each other. It's supposed to stop us from feeling lonely."

"You sound doubtful."

"I miss Earth. Isn't it crazy? In spite of the shortages, the overcrowding, the awful boredom of knowing exactly what every day is going to be like, in spite of everything I miss Earth."

"I don't see what there could be to miss."

"Oh, I miss the warm yellow sun and the moon. The things I always took for granted because they were always there. And I miss the sea. Our city wasn't far from the sea, and once in a while we used to get a day off to go there. The beaches were packed solid with people all the time, but still . . . the sea was so huge and empty and it had such a sound! I'll miss the sound of the sea."

"Some day perhaps you'll start a colony on the other side of Isis. There is ocean there, you know. I've never been there myself, though I've seen videos of it, of course. And don't you think, Mark, that the mountains are a bit like the sea. Look how they roll away into the distance. And when we have a storm you can hear the mountains roar as the wind rushes over them. It is marvellously exciting!"

"I've heard about the storms on Isis." Mark shivered. "Exciting doesn't seem to be the right word. But it's hard to believe in storms today. It's so beautiful and peaceful up here. It's a shame that it shouldn't be habitable."

"What do you mean? It *is*. Look at Guardian and me. We live up here. Of course we came here because of the Light, because the Light has to be as high and as far from inter-ference as possible. But we're perfectly comfortable, and, you know, I don't even like going down in the valley very much. The air down there is so thick and muggy it's like trying to breathe soup!"

He stared at her, and then said slowly. "Well, I suppose over the years you've become partly acclimatized. But even so, I just can't see spending the better part of my life in a UVO suit, breathing bottled oxygen instead of real air. The view is marvellous—I think upper Isis is the most beautiful place I've ever seen, but . . . well, I certainly wouldn't want to live up here. I need to feel the air on my skin, be free to breathe on my own."

"But I do. I am. Do you think that this suit is ultra-violet-opaque? Do you think I'm hiding an oxygen cylinder somewhere in here?" She stood up and stretched her arms to the sky. "No, Mark. I'm free of all that. Isis is mine and it can never harm me in any way. Guardian told me that when I was very little, and it's always been true. So perhaps when you have been here for a while you won't have to bother with all that stuff—suits and oxygen."

As Mark looked at her, with her arms stretched up towards the sun in a gesture of spontaneous happiness, he had to believe that she meant what she said, that she was not playing games. He remembered vaguely being taught that the Andean Indians were acclimatized to high altitudes after centuries of living there. The conquering Spaniards were able to survive, but in the thin atmosphere their wives could not bear healthy children, and so in the long run the Indians won.

"It takes generations to adapt like that," he argued, and she turned and looked down at him.

"I'm here." She shrugged and turned away, angry at his disbelief.

He said nothing more on the subject, but he thought about what she had said all the way down the dizzy 'stone staircase' and along the pebbly riverbank to the village. He lay awake that night thinking of Olwen, her arms stretched out to the cruel white sun.

Next afternoon he managed to get himself assigned to helping Doctor Phil put shelves and partitions into the newly built hospital. "How long do you think it'll take us to get acclimatized to upper Isis?" he asked when they took a breather.

"*Upper*? You're a bit impatient, aren't you, Mark? How about becoming acclimatized to lower Isis first."

"No, seriously. I need to know."

"Then, seriously, it would take a century or two of skilled

selective breeding. If we had a large population here you would get an adaptation to high altitudes as a result of the survival of the fittest . . . but not so long as we have UVO suits and oxygen to protect us. Anyway, that natural kind of genetic drift takes tens of centuries."

"Olwen told me that she could live on upper Isis without any protection."

"She's putting you on, Mark. So, she was born here. People have been born in undersea habitats, but that doesn't make them fish! Her parents must have had to protect her from the sun and from anoxia, from the moment she began to crawl."

"It's funny you should mention her parents. You know, she never has, not once. It's always Guardian. Guardian this and Guardian that!"

"Jealous?"

"Oh, don't be ridiculous! As if I'd be jealous of . . . but listen, Phil. She lives halfway up the mesa. I found the air was so thin even there that I started getting spots in front of my eyes when I breathed without an oxygen assist."

"I don't know why or how she lives up there. All I can say is, with absolute certainty, that it's a physiological impossibility for a human to live for long periods of time at such altitudes. I don't want to call the Keeper a liar. Maybe she's got a different concept of word-meanings than we do. But I'll tell you this. That fancy suit of hers *is* UVO, and she's got an oxygen supply of some kind in it, or I'll . . . I'll eat my Hippocratic oath! Now take this sketch over to Peter McCann for me, will you, and see if he can put me together a set of shelves from that stuff that looks like bamboo."

Mark had finished his errand and was on his way back to the hospital when he saw the tall figure of Guardian stalking down the river's edge towards the village. He had not returned since the day when Olwen had formally greeted the settlers, and Mark stared at him curiously as he walked towards the houses. Had Olwen come with him? He looked upstream, shading his eyes to stare at the side of the mesa where her home was.

It was hard to see anything from this distance. He could make out the balustrade of the terrace, though from here it looked like a natural fault in the rock. There was no sign of Olwen, no movement of any kind, and he felt a sudden surge of disappointment that stopped him dead in his tracks. What was going on? This was ridiculous. Here he was in a new and exciting world, with a lifetime of work to do, and all the room in the world in which to do it; and he was standing around thinking of this blessed girl. It was as bad as being in love.

Love? That was crazy, completely absolutely off. I've never even really *seen* her, he told himself angrily. Just talked to her . . . shared some thoughts . . . felt . . . felt what? Oh, idiot!

He came to himself, standing stock still in the middle of the compound, with Trudel, one of the girls of his ten, staring at him curiously. Blushingly he hurried back to the hospital. Just how long had he been standing there like a love-sick idiot?

The outside door of the hospital was closed, and he could hear Phil's voice. He hesitated with his hand on the latch. Could the doctor have a patient? The inside doors and partitions weren't finished yet and there was little privacy inside. Perhaps he should wait out here.

Another voice over-rode Phil's, unmistakably the Guardian's. His eyebrows raised in surprise, Mark pushed open the door. The two of them were standing in Phil's unfinished office. Neither of them noticed him. Their conversation— really, it was more like an argument—was too intense.

". . . no right to take blood samples without my permission," Guardian practically shouted.

"No right? Let me remind you that I am the physician in charge of *all* personnel on Isis. No exceptions. Who the hell do you think you are?" Phil shouted back.

"I am Guardian. Would you care to hear the tape on which I recorded Olwen's mother's dying words? She committed the child to my care, and I gave her my solemn promise to guard and protect the child. I have kept that promise, Doctor MacDonald, and I will go on keeping it. Neither you nor anyone else has the power to stop me."

Phil ran his hands through his hair and took a deep breath, more of a snort. The Guardian should have known better than to question the ethics of a red-headed Scottish physician, Mark thought, and waited for the explosion. He knew he had no right to eavesdrop, but argued to himself that he was just standing by in case the Guardian decided to get physical and Phil needed a helping hand.

The explosion didn't come. "I'm sure you mean well," the doctor kept his voice calm with a supreme effort. "But I insist that you are being illogically overprotective in keeping Olwen away from us, and isolating her in that ridiculous suit."

"I am never illogical," the Guardian interrupted grandly. "You overstepped your authority grossly in making those tests. I demand that you return the blood samples to me at once."

"I most certainly will not."

"Do you want to destroy Olwen?"

"Destroy? Of course I don't. Guardian, what am I going to find in those blood samples that you don't want me to see? If you are hiding something, remember that it may affect the future of the whole colony. Is it a virus? Something native to Isis that Olwen carries in her bloodstream? That's it, isn't it?"

Phil moved so abruptly that he knocked over a pile of boxes. The Guardian never flinched, but Mark, standing just inside the door, moved involuntarily. The doctor turned and saw him. "Oh. Mark. Back already? Would you find work in one of the other units for the rest of the afternoon?"

"I think I had better stay, don't you?" Mark walked forward, squaring his shoulders and clenching his fists.

"What? Oh, you're worried about the Guardian? Don't be. I'm fine, Mark. Off you go."

As Mark went out, feeling irritatingly younger than his seventeen years, he heard the doctor say roughly, "As for you, I think you had better tell me exactly what's been going on, and what you are trying to hide from us."

Mark walked idly across the compound, trying to make sense out of the fragments of conversation he had overheard. There was danger. That was the only thing that was really clear. Phil MacDonald was not merely angry. He was afraid. But not of the Guardian.

What else was there to be afraid of? The landing and the settlement had been carefully programmed and computer-vetted. Everything was going just as planned. Nothing had gone wrong. Really, on the whole of Isis there was only one unknown quantity, and that was Olwen herself. So it must be Olwen that was in danger. It would take a threat to *her* to bring the Guardian storming down from his heights. Do you want to destroy Olwen? He had asked Phil. Destroy? As if they would. The *Keeper*? None of it made any sense at all.

He was under orders to find work in another unit, but Phil hadn't specified where. He squinted up at Ra. It was in the west, but there were a few hours of light left. He would have to make up his mind fast, before someone noticed that he was doing nothing, and handed him something to hold or carry.

Quickly he ducked into stores, where luckily nobody was about, and picked up a UVO suit and oxygen outfit. He made them into as inconspicuous a roll as he could, tucked the roll under his arm, and walked purposefully out of stores, across the compound and up river towards the Cascades. He did not stop until a bend in the river and a flank of rock hid him from the sight of the village.

He undid his bundle, struggled into the suit, clipped the oxygen cylinder into place and put on the face mask. He had to talk to Olwen and find out exactly what kind of danger she was in. If he only knew, there must be something he could do to help.

It was a long haul up to the house, but not as bad as before. His muscles must be getting into practise at last. He was panting, but not exhausted, when he reached the terrace.

It was deserted. The chairs and hammock were empty. But there was a half-finished drink on one of the small tables, and a book of verse jammed down so carelessly that one of the pages had been bent over. He straightened it carefully before closing it and putting it back on the table.

He stopped at the door to the house and stripped off his face-mask. "Olwen?" There was no answer. "OLWEN! Are you there? Are you all right?"

Silence answered him. An overpoweringly beautiful scent drifted through the cool dark room. It came from a table near the window, from a single golden flower floating in a hand-

56

blown glass bowl. He looked round, breathing at his mask as he felt the need to yawn, to get more air.

Elegant furniture, hand-carved, polished. A rich carpet in front of the fireplace. What was it? The fur of some exotic Isis animal, or a synthetic dreamed up by the Guardian himself? Mark walked on tiptoe across the room. He had never in his life seen such beauty and elegance close enough to touch, and it awed him.

At the back of the living room there were two doors. He called, listened, pushed the first one open. A kitchen, bright, functional and shiningly clean. A drift of cooking smell from a pot on the stove made his mouth salivate. In the second room were rows of computers, radio equipment, TV monitors. Beyond them, a glimpse of a white-tiled laboratory. This was obviously the domain of the Guardian.

When he had returned to the living room he noticed a passage leading away to his left, and he followed it, marvelling at how the house had been hewn from the living rock, the wall and floors smoothed and sprayed with plastic to an almost mirror finish. The passage ended and a curtained archway opened on to a room to his right. It was Olwen's room. He knew it as soon as he had pushed aside the filmy curtain. He couldn't bring himself to put even one foot on the soft white carpet. He stood in the archway and called her name again.

There was no sound except for his beating heart. The sight of the quiet spring-like room had made his chest feel suddenly two sizes too small for his heart. He could feel her presence in the empty room, and he had a sudden insane impulse to cross the white carpet and fling himself down on that pink-frilled bed, to feel close to her. What was the matter with him? He shook his head, took a deep breath of oxygen, and blundered clumsily across the living room and onto the terrace again.

In the harsh glare of Ra's light, reflected off the eastern mountains, sanity returned. He licked his dry lips, and impulsively drank the fruit juice from the glass on the table. It had an unearthly tang, part fruity, part resinous, but it quenched his thirst and cleared his head. He leaned back against the stone balustrade and craned his neck up towards the top of the mesa.

She must be up there. Where else would she be likely to go? Dared he risk the climb alone? He felt suddenly reckless and ready to dare anything. Perhaps there was something in that odd drink. Or perhaps it was the memory of the urgency in the Guardian's voice . . . Do you want to destroy Olwen?

Without giving himself any more time to think about it, Mark set his foot into the first lasered notch in the rock face and began to climb. In a way it was more difficult this time. He had to search out for himself every notch, crevice and knob that was to give him toe and finger hold. But in another way it was easier. He could go at his own speed, not trying to compete with a nimble girl who could climb like a goat or a spider.

He climbed slowly, making no mistakes, taking his time. He was in much better shape today, hardly more than out of breath by the time he felt the familiar cool air that seemed to slide off the flat top of the mesa to meet him. One more big stretch. Both arms around that pinnacle of rock. And he was there, on top, triumphant!

It was worth it. Olwen was there, standing into the wind as if she were a part of it, looking west towards the sun, towards the rolling sea of red and purple mountain. Her back was towards him. She was wearing a long dress of some fine silvery stuff that seemed to change colours as the wind moved it, the way opal does, or mother-of-pearl. Her hair was loose, cascading down her back in a rich torrent of coppery red.

Mark knelt at the edge of the mesa, his right arm still resting on the rock by which he had hauled himself up. "Oh, you beauty," he said under his breath. He knew that she was the most lovely, the most graceful, the most desirable woman he would ever see in his whole life.

She was like Isis as she stood there. She was alien, like the wonderful tangy drink, like the scented golden flower, like the rolling mountains. She was like Ra, shining intensely blue-white, pure energy. She was like the night sky, pulsing with stars in the pattern of an as yet unknown but captivating dance.

"Olwen." He spoke again. This time she heard him and

turned in a sudden swirl of coppery hair and opalescent drapery.

Mark staggered to his feet and took one totally involuntary step backward. There was nothing there. He grabbed at the rock. His fingers caught for an instant. He felt the roughness sliding past his skin. He was going over backwards into space. He felt himself fall. Felt the breath jolt from his body as it hit the first outcrop and bounced free. Then there was nothing but blackness and a sense of irrational horror.

Chapter Six

Olwen was furious with Guardian. She had felt edgy all day, trying to paint, to read, unable to settle down to anything. Tomorrow she and Mark had planned to climb up past the Cascades. She wanted . . . what did she want? She asked Guardian once again to let her meet Mark without having to wear the suit and face-mask, which were becoming more and more obnoxious to her, and once again he refused.

"It is not like you to be so illogical," he said, and she snapped back.

"It is not like you to refuse me something so important."

"What can be so important about a suit? It is comfortable, is it not? It fits well?"

"Oh, you just don't understand!" She threw her book down and ran her fingers through her hair, feeling totally frustrated. She walked across the terrace and stood with her back to him, staring across the river valley to the eastern mountains. Her skin felt twitchy, her stomach knotted in a very uncomfortable way, and she suddenly wanted to cry.

"Then explain it to me." Guardian's patient voice behind her was the last straw. If only he would be angry or rude or unkind or *something*. He was always so right. She picked up a flower vase and threw it at him, hard; but even that was an ineffectual gesture. He fielded the ornament neatly and put it down carefully and without haste on a nearby table.

"OH!!!" She stamped her foot and whirled past him, across the living room and into the privacy of her own room. She flung herself face down on her bed and began to cry angrily.

After a time her anger seemed to melt away, but she still went on crying. I must be the most unhappy person in the

60

whole galaxy, she thought, with a certain melancholy pleasure, and she let the tears well up in her eyes and trickle down into her pillow. But eventually the pillow became uncomfortably damp, and she turned it and herself over. Lying on her back seemed to turn off the rest of her tears. Her legs and arms felt limp and soft, and she was almost ready to go to sleep. She sighed and blew her nose.

"Olwen, may I come in?"

"Why?" She rolled over on her elbow and looked at Guardian hovering in the doorway.

"I would like to examine you. I am afraid you may be ill."

"There's nothing wrong with me."

"Then why were you crying?"

She thought about it. She'd never wanted to cry before, not like that. "I suppose because I wanted to."

"Can you tell me why?"

"I'm not sure I know."

"Perhaps I should psychoanalyse you."

"I'm all right." She sat up cross-legged on the bed and blew her nose again. "I just don't want to wear that beastly suit and mask again. That's all."

"But why? I have explained . . ."

"I want Mark to see *me*, to know *me*, not a plastic imitation," she burst out. "Anyway Doctor MacDonald thinks you're wrong. He says the settlers have no viruses or bacteria that could possibly hurt me."

"He could be wrong, Olwen. It is a matter of opinion."

"No, it's not. It's a matter of fact—or will be, very soon. The doctor took a sample of my blood and he's going to make cultures of it, and in a few days he's going to be able to prove to you that I don't have to wear that stupid suit, so there!"

"He did *what*!" In two strides Guardian was across the room. He grasped her arms, pushing the light sleeves back. He stared at the little mark where the needle had gone in. Then, without saying another word, he dropped her arms, turned and stalked out of the room.

"Where are you going? What's the matter?" Olwen had never seen Guardian behave as if he were actually angry, and it scared her. He would not answer, and she bounced off the

61

bed and followed him across the living room and onto the terrace. "Guardian, please. Talk to me. Where are you going? What are you going to do? I'm sorry I was cross and threw that vase at you. Please talk to me."

He turned at the head of the stairs that led down to the river. "I am going to see Doctor MacDonald." His voice was as calm as ever. Perhaps she had imagined the anger.

"Don't go. Please let it be. Don't stop him."

Guardian shook his head. "You should never have interfered, Olwen. You should have left well enough alone. You know in your heart that I want what is best for you—that that is all that I have ever wanted."

She began to cry again. "You don't understand. I *love* Mark." It wasn't until she had actually said it that she realised that it was the truest and most important thing she had ever said. "I love Mark," she said again slowly. "I want him to see *me*. To get to know *me*. The reason for the suit was just pretend, wasn't it? It has nothing to do with germs. It was something you dreamed up to keep us apart, just so this wouldn't happen."

"Believe me, Olwen, the suit was never pretence—not in the way you mean. It was essential. It *is* essential."

"For what?"

"Your happiness. That is my chief imperative. Surely you know that by now?" He did not wait for an answer, but began to climb down the stairs to the valley below.

She leaned over the balustrade and shouted after him. "If you want to make me happy, then don't go to Doctor MacDonald. Let him finish the tests. I promise you I'll abide by his decision."

Guardian shook his head. "I know you will. And that is why I must go and see him."

She watched the upright figure grow smaller and smaller as he neared the valley bottom, and then began to walk purposefully towards the village. Her hands gripped the balustrade until her fingers hurt. There was nothing so infuriating as a totally logical person, especially when what they were doing made no sense at all.

She felt a sudden longing for the open sky and the wind against her body. Without bothering to go back inside and

62

change into a jumpsuit, more suitable for climbing, she wrapped the loose hem of her long dress around her waist, tucked in the end securely, and began to climb to the top of the mesa.

Up there was freedom and peace. The strong northwest wind blew her red hair out behind her, and tugged at her gown until the hem came loose again, and it drifted out behind her like a silver spider's web. She stood as close as she could to the northwest edge, ignoring the plunging depths below, feeling the wind buffet her skin. It pressed against her body like a living thing. She felt, as she had often felt before up here, that with but the tiniest effort on her part she would be able to fly, to mount the rising air currents, to soar like a hawk on the updraught that rose in a tangible wave above the side of the mesa.

She raised her arms, felt the wind take them. It had blown from the far sea, across range after range of mountain, and now it smelled of the spring cactus flower, heady as honey, and it was spicy with dry mountain grass and the scent of the aromatic oil that oozed from the thorn bushes as Ra grew hotter.

Olwen looked northwest, across the illimitable ranges of Isis. She felt as if she were at the prow of a great ship, cutting its way through a purplish-red swell, sailing on and on around the planet. She was at the same time the captain and the figure-head. The prow of the mesa cleft the wind. The wind strengthened and shook the cactuses. The noise filled her ears.

She never heard Mark. Not until he called her name . . .

It was like the chiming of a bell in a perfect time and a perfect place. She knew, with a sure sense of peace, that he loved her as she loved him, that it was going to be all right. Slowly she lowered her arms and turned, smiling, and walked across the width of the mesa top towards him.

What happened next went by so fast that between the time she had drawn one breath and let it out again it was all over. Yet in some way that she could not understand she could see it all, she went on seeing it all, as if it were a series of photographs being flipped over in front of her eyes, to give a jerky imitation of life.

Flip. Mark, kneeling on the grass at the top of the path up to the mesa, his arm on the boulder which stood at the north side of the path.

Flip. Mark, standing suddenly, his arms up and out in front of him. Stiff. Even the fingers stiff, as if he were pushing away something invisible that was in front of his face.

Flip. Mark, taking a great step backwards, where there was no step to take.

Flip. Mark, his arms flung suddenly above his head, disappearing out of sight down the far side of the mesa.

The breath she let out was a scream. "Mark, look out!" But it was already too late. He had already taken that huge horrifying step. That was how quickly it had all happened.

She flung herself across the top of the mesa, her robe clinging to knees and ankles, getting in her way. Desperately she reached down and tore at it until the material ripped away and her legs were free.

From the top of the path she could not even see him. An enormous shudder welled up inside and shook her body. She forced her eyes down, down to the scree that littered the grey grassland at the foot of the mesa. Red scree. The colour of a broken body. Her eyes searched the shadows frantically, but she still could not see him. The path descended to the left, in a slightly northerly direction. In his fall Mark would have gone straight down. But how far?

She went cautiously down the trail, for the first time in her life afraid of the height, aware of the cruel depths. Instead of being friends, the rocks that were familiar hand and foot holds had suddenly become enemies. Each time she had to trust her weight to them she did not really trust. She could feel her heart pounding against her chest wall. Her bare hands were slippery with perspiration.

She was halfway down the trail to the house before she saw him. He was half-sprawled, half-dangling, in a tiny horizontal fault where a meagre thorn bush grew. As she left the path and slithered across the rock-face towards him she could smell the aromatic scent, pungent where his fallen body had bruised the thin grey leaves. When she was close enough to reach out and touch him, she could see that the only thing holding him against the cliff was the harness of his oxygen supply, which had caught on a tiny spur of rock. Though the thorn bush clung to his suit it was itself too small and brittle to be of any help.

Mark's face-mask had been torn off in the fall and dangled just below him. His lips were blue, but she told herself that he was still breathing. She dared not touch him in case he slipped. All she could do was to reach down for the dangling mask and place it lightly against his face. Then she waited, clinging to the fault with toes and fingernails, as close to Mark as she could get without touching him.

Over and over through her mind ran the inexplicable event. Flip. Flip. Flip. Flip. Over and over.

Ra moved down the sky. The top of the mesa cast a shadow across the river valley and half way up the flank of the eastern mountains. Flip. Flip. Flip. Flip.

A thousand years went by. At last she saw Guardian, walking purposefully from the village towards the foot of the Cascades. He was so slow. Why hadn't he taken a floater, instead of choosing to walk? She yelled, but an updraught of warm air from the valley grasslands took her voice and threw it at the sky. Very carefully she moved away from Mark, dug into the fault with her fingernails until she was able to pry out a small stone. Carefully, very carefully, the sweat running down her face, she moved her arm and threw it.

It was not very close, but it·was close enough for his keen ears. Anyone else might have ignored the sound of the gently ricocheting stone, but not Guardian. He looked up, scanned the cliff-face, and saw them. Slowly Olwen let out her breath.

He crossed the river and came up the precipitous side of the mesa like a tank, and as soon as he was close enough for Olwen to hear him he told her to get back to the path and go home. "Radio the village and warn the doctor to be prepared. Then have a floater ready for me."

She nodded and scrambled her way back to the path, her mouth dry with fear. She dared not look behind her to see whether Guardian could unhook Mark without sending the two of them down the side of the mesa onto the sharp-edged scree. All she could do was trust that Guardian could manage it, and hurry down to the house to do as she was told.

She pulled a floater out so that it stood close to the south end of the terrace. She raised the village on the radio, and reached the terrace again, with an armful of blankets, as Guardian came down the last few steps, slid Mark carefully from his shoulder and placed him on the floater.

Olwen dropped to her knees beside him and held his cold hand. "Is he. . . ?" She could not bear to say the word.

"He's still alive." Guardian checked him with careful hands and placed the oxygen mask more securely. "Broken ribs. Maybe internal injuries. I will take him down to Doctor MacDonald and stay to help if I am needed."

"Let me come too," she begged. She could not let go of Mark's hand. She felt as if it were *her* heart pumping blood through his body, *her* lungs forcing him to breathe. How could she possibly let go?

"You must." Guardian was stern. He strapped Mark in, climbed into the driver's seat and switched on the engine. "Let go, Olwen."

"I can't."

"You're not thinking of Mark. You're thinking of yourself."

She let go the limp hand then, and the floater rose and hovered at balustrade level. "But what can I do to help," she wailed.

"Pray," said Guardian, and let the floater drop down valley, down river. In less than a minute he had landed it neatly outside the new hospital. The lights were on down there. Olwen saw the tiny figures scurrying around, saw Mark, like a broken dolls' house figure, lifted onto a stretcher and carried into the hospital.

She let go of the balustrade and walked slowly into the house. The living room was filled with the heady perfume of the golden cactus flower. She hated the scent. It was sweet. Overpoweringly sweet. For the rest of her life she would remember this day every time she smelled its scent. Every spring. She lifted the flower carefully out of its bowl and dropped it into the kitchen incinerator.

Flip. Flip. Flip. Flip. The pictures flicked through her mind. The scent of the flower clung to her hands. She went

66

through her bedroom to her bathroom and scrubbed and scrubbed until there was no vestige of scent left. She noticed her dress, torn and filthy, its skirt half ripped off, and she took it off and put on a dressing gown, wrapping it tightly round her as if the warmth could comfort her.

Flip. Flip. Flip. Flip. As she lay on her bed and stared dry-eyed at the ceiling the pictures appeared in front of her eyes. She shut her eyes tightly. Put her hands over them.

Flip. Flip. Flip. Flip. They were still there, inside her brain. She pushed her hands into her temples as if she could force the memory out of her mind.

Guardian had told her to pray. When she was little he had explained to her about God, and taught her how to pray. But the God he had taught her about was the One who had set the stars in the sky to blaze in His glory. He had made Ra and Isis and the beautiful mountains. The great lights of the aurora, and the pungent thorn bushes and the sweet golden cactus flower.

She faltered. Flip. Flip. Flip. Flip. The new automatic memory took over her brain again. She forced the pictures away. Guardian had never told her about a God who could do a thing like that to Mark. It was not fair. They loved each other. They had been born five parsecs apart and some miracle had brought them together to love each other. It was as if God had made a beautiful jewel for her, and then just as she had reached out for it, He had slapped her hand aside, broken it and sent the pieces flying. How could she pray to that kind of God?

She lay and stared at the ceiling. The light in the room dimmed from clear blue-white daylight to a soft purplish glow, as Ra's last rays were reflected into her room from the eastern mountains across the valley. Then even that light vanished as Ra sank below the horizon.

One by one the stars pricked out in the dark sky, until they made a blaze above the black line of the mountains. A long time after that she heard the hum of the returning floater. She was out of her room and across the living room before Guardian's silhouette showed in the doorway.

Quite suddenly the nervous energy that had kept her strung, wide awake, unmindful of the passing hours, seemed

67

to shut itself off. She felt her knees go soft under her and she had to grab the back of a chair to stop herself from falling to the floor. She tried to talk, but nothing came out but a despairing little croak. In two strides Guardian had crossed the room, picked her up and propped her up on the sofa close to the fire. The fire was lit, she was wrapped in a warm blanket, given a hot drink. She couldn't swallow, but she held the mug close, warming her icy hands.

"Mark is going to be all right," Guardian assured her. "He has a couple of broken ribs and there was some internal bleeding. But he has had surgery and all is now well."

"Truly?"

"I have never lied to you before, have I, Olwen?"

She shook her head. "I couldn't pray," she told him. "I felt so . . . so angry."

"It is all right. He will understand."

Comforted, she was able to sip the hot drink. In ten minutes her eyelids were so heavy that she could not keep them open. She struggled, and through the flickering lids saw Guardian standing above her. Something in his attitude made Olwen sure that he was guarding her from some unknown peril or pain. What could it be?

She tried to ask him what it was, but sleep was stronger than curiosity, and when she opened her eyes again it was halfway through the next morning. The sun was pouring through the deep stone windows and she had forgotten all about the curious incident.

She was starving. She felt as hollow as if she hadn't eaten for days, and when she thought about it she realised that indeed she'd had nothing since yesterday's breakfast, and she had not been in the mood to eat it. Guardian was nowhere to be seen, so she went into the kitchen and got herself together a meal of cold fish and bamboo shoots and fruit, and took it all out onto the terrace to eat.

One of the floaters was missing. For a moment she had a twinge of fear. Was Mark worse? But Guardian had promised. She remembered that, the last foggy thought before sleep. Guardian had promised that all would be well.

She took the empty dishes back to the kitchen and then had a long shower and washed her hair. It seemed very important to look her best. Perhaps today they would let her see Mark . . .

She was sitting on the terrace drying her hair and trying to concentrate on a book when Guardian returned. She jumped up. "Mark?"

"He is healing well."

"When may I visit him?"

Guardian hesitated, as if searching for the right words. "It would not be advisable."

"Right now. I understand. But when. . . ?"

"Perhaps not at all."

"Not. . . ? But I *love* him."

"I know. It is very difficult for you." Again the hesitation.

She stared. "Doesn't Mark *want* to see me?" she asked sharply. It was strange how all her senses seemed to be heightened. She was aware as never before of the incredible clarity of the still air. She could see a sky-lark, high, unbelievably high, and catch every note of its faint piercing song. She could feel the fabric of her jumpsuit against her skin, the rough-smooth of the bamboo canes of her chair. She could smell, separate and identify a dozen scents at once.

And she could read Guardian, as she had never been able to read him before. There was not much. A micro-second's hesitation. Something different in the inflection of his words, as if he were skating on the edge of truth.

"Doesn't Mark want to see me?" she asked again.

"The doctor feels it would not be wise. From what Mark said in delirium."

"Mark loves me."

"He does not know you, as you know him."

"I know he loves me," she affirmed proudly. "He does . . . doesn't he?"

Guardian lifted his hands. "How can you truly love what you do not know?"

"You take it on faith," she blurted out, and pushed the back of her hand against her eyes. "*I* did."

"You are something special," he said softly.

"But you're trying to tell me that Mark doesn't . . . is that it?"

"He will later. When he knows you properly. The real

69

you. You must not be so impatient."

"We've got so little time. Don't you understand? A life-time isn't enough. Not nearly. To go on knowing . . . to be close to . . ." The tears ran down her face and she couldn't stop them. She jumped to her feet and ran to the edge of the terrace, to stare down into the foaming cauldron at the bottom of the Cascades.

Guardian made a swift movement towards her. "Olwen!"

She turned to stare at the tone of his voice. "Oh, I'm not going to throw myself over, if that's what you're thinking. It's all right. I won't do anything . . . I've got to walk . . . to be by myself. That's all."

He nodded. "Where will you go? To the mesa top?"
She shuddered and shook her head, wondering if she would ever be able to go up there again, without having to relive that long second in which Mark fell backwards out of sight, a look of horror in his eyes that she could see even through the tinted face-plate of his breathing mask.

"I'll go down there somewhere." She waved her hand in a vaguely southerly direction across the plain.

"The valley? You dislike the valley. Why would you choose to go there?"

She shrugged. "I don't know. I don't want to climb. Does it matter?"

"Will you wear your suit, Olwen?"

"No!"

"Will you promise to keep a safe distance away from any of the settlers."

"Don't worry, Guardian. I don't want to see them now. It's only Mark I want to see. It's only Mark I ever want to see."

She began to climb down the stone staircase to the valley floor, quickly, before he could think of any other objections. It was strange. She had never wanted to get away from Guardian before, but now everything he said and did seemed to set her teeth on edge so that she wanted to scream.

At the foot of the mesa she struck off as far to the west of south as she could, giving the lake and the village a wide berth. It had been still all morning, but now the wind was rising. Soon there would be one of Isis' dramatic spring storms. At the moment it was just enough to flatten the grass blooms, so that it seemed to Olwen that she was walking waist-high in a rose and silver sea that washed in living waves around her.

After an hour she had walked far to the west, leaving the scorched landing spot where Pegasus Two still squatted behind and to her left. She strode along, heedless of everything, the quietness slowly stilling the turmoil in her mind.

A sudden yammering noise made her heart pound, and before she was fully aware of what had happened an enormous hairy shape bounded down the flank of the mesa and flung itself on top of her. She staggered back and sat down with a jolt that made her gasp. Hobbit! He stood above her, both front paws planted firmly on her shoulders, licking her face with his enormous rasping tongue. He had never been so demonstrative before, not even as a lonely little puppy; and she realised guiltily that she had completely ignored him since the landing of Pegasus Two.

"I'm sorry." She spoke into the fur of his long neck as she hugged him, carefully avoiding the spiny bits of his neck. "I've been a beast. You've always been my friend . . . my only friend except for Guardian . . . since they came I've just ignored you."

Hobbit sat back and panted, his long purple tongue hanging out between two rows of inch-long fangs, his little slanty red eyes full of affection. "I *do* love you," Olwen explained. "You are the best playmate a person could have. I just got carried away. I'm sorry. Do you want to play now?"

Hobbit huffed, jumped up off all four feet at once and bounded off, vanishing into the long grass in the general direction of the rocket-site. He was back in a while with a long stick in his mouth. It must have belonged to the settlers, since it was of smooth wood, painted in black and white stripes.

"I have the distinct feeling that you shouldn't have taken that," Olwen told him as she turned it over in her hands. "But then they're messing up my whole beautiful Isis. Let's hope they don't grudge one stick." She flung it from her, high in the air, so that it turned slowly end over end before plummeting into the long grass.

Hobbit stiffened, roared and rushed after it. Faintly, back towards the landing site, Olwen heard voices, and mindful of Guardian's warning, and not anxious to meet any of the new settlers herself, she turned towards the mesa, away from the grassy valley.

Hobbit bounded triumphantly back to her, the stick between his massive jaws. He pushed it against her chest until she took it from him and threw it again. It went into the long grass, back the way they had come, and she went on walking among the boulders and bushes that covered the lower flanks of Lighthouse Mesa, her thoughts on Mark. He *must* love her. It was the others, trying to keep them apart . . .

Only too soon Hobbit was back, yammering joyfully. Again she threw the stick, high and as far as she could. Perhaps this time it would take him longer to find. She loved Hobbit, but she needed the peace to think out her own muddled thoughts without the constant interruption of his noisy boisterousness.

She reached the place where the mesa curved northward to become the western side of Cascade Valley. She could hear Hobbit snuffling and baying, and the swooshing noise of his passage through the long grass. Further off she could hear men's voices. They were excited, shouting. Perhaps they were hunting game. There were many small deer-like creatures that lived in the long grass. Guardian had proper names for them all, but she had never named them. Somehow to name things that might later turn up in a stew or a soup was rather horrible, and she kept her names only for friends like Hobbit, or for the dear little jumping dormice that lived in burrows all over the top of the mesa.

A shot rang out, much closer than she had expected from the distance and direction of the voices. Well, they had got their dinner then. Food for the settlement. In an abstract way she was glad for them.

She walked on. The river and the mesa wall began to crowd each other. She was nearly home. She turned to call Hobbit. It would be safer for him up on the mesa or in the mountains.

There was no answer. The grass was still, except where the wind flattened it like a giant's hand gently touching. "Hobbit!" she shouted again. Then a sudden chill ran down

72

her body and she tore back across the rough scree-strewn slope. She hadn't far to go. He had almost caught up with her. He lay just where the deep grass started, on his side, the stupid striped stick beside him where his slackened jaw had dropped it.

Frantically she knelt down beside him and called his name. The slanty red eyes opened and looked at her. Then, slowly, as if he were very tired, the tongue came up and gave her face one lick. There was a great wound in his side, and she tore at her scarf, wadding it and putting over the wound, pressing, pressing. Only it wasn't nearly big enough, and the blood bubbled up between her fingers no matter how hard she tried to push it back.

Then it stopped, and for a miraculous second she thought that she had won; until she looked into the empty eyes and saw that her friend Hobbit had gone away for ever. She bent her head over his body and wept, for Hobbit, for herself, for Isis.

She was still sitting there with his head in her lap when the hunters burst out of the long grass. "Murderers! Beasts!" she screamed at them. "Get out of here. You've killed him. You've killed my Hobbit. Go away. Get out. Get off my planet!" She picked up the striped stick and threw it at them.

The shock of her accusation was mirrored in the stunned and horrified expressions in their faces. Then, in a completely incomprehensible gesture, one of them pulled out his hand-gun and pointed it at *her*. She stared without moving, too stunned to react. And in the next second the other man had knocked his hand to the side and pulled him away. They both turned then and ran, making a broad swathe of trampled grass back towards the lake.

Olwen did not cry any more. She laid her head against Hobbit's neck, and lovingly remembered every incident of their life together, from the day when Guardian had first brought him to the house as a squalling hungry half-metre-long pup.

It is all my fault, she thought miserably. He was a mountain animal. He only came down into the grassland after me because he was lonely, because I'd been neglecting him . . . thinking about Mark. And he was faithful to me, was

Hobbit, all of his life, up to the last loving second.

After a while she got stiffly to her feet and walked slowly towards the river. She forded it just above the lake and turned south towards the village. She was unaware of the blood that covered her hands and stained the front of her jumpsuit. She walked along very slowly, holding her anger like something precious.

The two hunters must have already warned the others, because the second she entered the village the women and children ran screaming into their houses and shut the doors. Only one child—she remembered him vaguely as the youngest—seemed not to be concerned and went on with what he was doing until a grey-faced man ran from one of the buildings and yanked him to his feet and pulled him indoors.

Olwen stood alone with her anger in the middle of the empty street. She picked up a stone and hurled it at the nearest window. It was plastic and the stone merely rebounded, leaving a white bruise on the transparent surface. She found a larger stone, almost a boulder, and threw it with every gram of strength. This time the whole window fell in with a satisfying crash. "I hate you!" she screamed at the blank empty hole. "You killed Hobbit. You're spoiling Isis. Go away. I don't need you here." She threw another stone. Another window fell. "Go back to Earth where you belong. Isis is mine. Mine."

She bent to pick up another stone, and then suddenly Guardian was beside her. She had not even heard his feet through her yells and the screams of the settlers. He picked her up as if she were still a child. "Put me *down!*" she shouted, and hammered as hard as she could at his shoulder and back with the stone she had just picked up. He did not falter. He turned and walked out of the village and up the valley towards the Cascades.

Olwen dropped the stone and began to cry. By the time they had reached the stairway to the house her tears had dissolved the rest of her anger away. "Please put me down. I can walk up."

Once on the terrace she was ashamed to meet his eye. "I'm so sorry," she whispered. "Did I hurt you most dreadfully?"

"Nothing that can't be fixed," he reassured her gently.

74

"This wasn't your fault, Olwen. None of it has been your fault. It is just that you did not understand. Dr MacDonald told me that I should have explained everything to you before ever Pegasus Two landed, but I . . ." he stopped and Olwen's eyes widened in alarm.

"What is it, Guardian? You *are* hurt."

"No." His voice was firm again. "I am torn two ways, which is a painfully illogical state. I did it all for your good and for your happiness, you see. But it has made you unhappy."

"What did you do? It wasn't your fault that those horrible settlers killed Hobbit. Oh, Guardian dear, will you please go back and find Hobbit's body for me, and bury it nicely, up on the mesa." Her voice trembled.

"Yes, Olwen. I will do it right away, while there is still some light. But later, after supper, we must talk, you and I. There is so much to tell you that you do not know, and I have much explaining to do."

He took the floater and went off down valley, and Olwen walked numbly into the house. She felt that she could not bear to watch for his return. Her hands were sticky. She looked down and saw all the blood and ripped off her clothes and threw them into the incinerator, and then stood under the shower, as if the warm water could wash away the pain, until she heard Guardian coming back into the house.

Chapter Seven

Mark was badly hurt, and Hobbit was dead. Nothing could ever be the same again. Olwen felt herself hurting as if it were her blood that stained the soil of Isis. She had turned to Guardian for comfort and found nothing but uncertainty. Uncertainty from *Guardian*? She tried to eat, though supper tasted like sand in her mouth; and while she pushed the food around her plate, cutting it into little pieces and hiding the pieces under a salad leaf, he fidgeted. Guardian?

Finally she pushed her plate away. "I'm sorry. I simply can't." And instead of scolding her he seemed relieved.

"Now we will talk. Now I can explain," he said, and led Olwen through into the signals room.

"Why here?" In spite of her numbness a mild curiosity stirred in her.

"Not here. Beyond." Guardian gestured, and in the far wall she noticed another door.

"I don't remember seeing this before. How odd. What is it?"

"Come and see." Guardian held the door for her, and she entered the strange room and looked around her curiously.

The room was totally impersonal. There were filing cabinets and cases of video-tape and micro-film. There was a computer terminal and consoles. Beyond a glass wall lay another room, white-tiled, with high tables networked with an intricate lace of glassware. It looked like a cross between an operating theatre and a chemical factory. This, then, must be where Guardian produced the new fabrics from Isis' raw materials, stuff for their furniture and clothes.

There was no bedroom, unless Guardian slept on that high sterile-looking slab in the white-tiled room. There were no personal mementos, no ornaments. The whole place was unattractive, chilly and somehow depressing.

"So this is where you spend your spare time, Guardian? Oh dear, it's so bleak. Why haven't you made it as nice for yourself as you've made the rest of the house?"

"You needed beauty to help you grow, Olwen. I do not. Everything I need I already have."

"Really?" Olwen turned slowly round. "It's funny. I don't ever remember noticing this door before, or coming through here, and yet I've been in the signals room every day of my life. How can that be?"

"It is nothing to be concerned about. In the beginning I gave you the post-hypnotic suggestion not to notice the door or come into this part of the house until I felt you were ready. Now the time has come. Will you sit here?"

He indicated a hard upright chair that stood in front of the computer screen. As she obeyed him Olwen wondered for a scared second if Guardian were about to punish her for throwing stones at the settlers. He hadn't said one word about it, not one word . . . She swallowed and sat down meekly.

Nothing like that happened. Guardian fussed about, almost as if he were nervous, and then dropped a tape into the video slot. There was a hum. Orange numbers danced sideways on a green background. The picture blurred and jumped suddenly into focus. A view of the lake with the grassland beyond. She could see that the trees were laden with fruit. The camera zoomed in among the leaves, and a woman's hand appeared and twisted off a fruit. The camera followed the fruit towards a woman's face . . . a woman with small neat features and a cloud of brown hair. Olwen had the tantalizing feeling that she should know her, and yet she was sure she had not seen her among the new settlers.

The woman laughed, bit into the fruit, and then slowly licked the juice off her fingers. Her lips moved, and though Olwen realised that she was talking to whoever it was who held the camera, her eyes looked straight into Olwen's, and it was just as if she were talking to *her*. It was tantalising that this tape had no audio.

Who could the woman be? Olwen suddenly realised that since the fruit was ripe it must be autumn. But there had been no one on Isis except for herself and Guardian for all the autumns of her life. And it definitely *was* Isis. The camera drew back and she could see the mesa with the lighthouse on its top, clear in the background behind the woman's head.

She turned to Guardian, a dozen questions bubbling up inside. Only he was not looking at her. He was watching the screen in a positively broody way. Whatever was to be explained, he was going to do it his way.

She turned back to the video screen. There were two people in the picture now. The woman had been joined by a man, tall and good-looking, slender, with a determinedly square chin. His eyes, as he looked fleetingly at the camera, were piercingly blue, and his hair was curly and red. He had his arm around the young woman. She was small; her head only came to the middle of his shoulder, Olwen noticed. He looked down at her with the nicest, most loving expression that was like the sky-lark song; it made Olwen hurt inside.

His lips moved, and she longed to be able to lip-read; and yet at the same time she had the odd feeling that whatever he was saying was private. The girl was so lovely, with high wide cheekbones, large dark eyes, and an expressive mouth that curled up at the corners, as if laughter was always bubbling just below the surface.

They turned and walked away from the camera towards a hut built of bamboo—a hut Olwen had never seen before, though she realised with a sort of shock that it occupied the exact place that the settlers had chosen for their village. They stopped at the door and turned for an instant. Don't go, she wanted to call to them. Please stay!

The scene dissolved into pictures of a baby, lying in a swinging bamboo cradle in the shade of the hut. Other sequences followed. Under Olwen's fascinated eyes the child grew, laughed, cried, slept, crawled, sucked its thumb, was tossed into the air, carried piggy-back, cuddled, and kissed, and finally stood up, staggered, walked, reached out to the camera.

In the last scene, before the screen blanked out, the child had grown to a sturdy toddler with a determined chin, deep blue eyes, and wavy hair that was an unusual shade of reddish brown.

78

"Guardian?" Olwen found that her voice was trembling. She had the strange feeling that she was standing on the brink of a fast deep river. She wanted desperately to go forward, and yet she was afraid. "Who are they? Where are they? Why have I never seen them before? Is it all real or just a story?"

"Look at me, Olwen." Guardian's voice resonated in the large cave-like room. She looked up obediently, and then went still. Like a fledgling bursting out of its shell her mind began to stir.

Her hands went up to her head. "Oh, it hurts! It hurts!"

"It is all right," he told her gently. "*Now* you will remember."

Her hands fell to her lap. She stared back at the blank screen. "My . . . my parents? My mother? My father? And the child was . . . me?"

Guardian nodded. "How do you feel about it?"

"I don't know. I have to think. I . . . why have I never asked you about my parents before? Why don't I remember them myself?"

"I wiped the memory from your mind. It seemed the kindest thing to do. I did not want you to grieve or to feel lonely without them."

"Grieve . . . ?"

"They died when you were four Earth-years old. There was a catastrophic storm, the worst there has ever been on Isis . . . one in a thousand years, perhaps. And at that time we were not prepared for it. They were both out on a geological survey, and I was at home with you."

"Here?"

"No. The house in the valley by the lake. I had built this cave to store the communications equipment. I brought you here and left you in an oxygenated crib while I went to look for Gareth and Liz. Gareth—your father—was already dead. I believe he had died instantly. He looked very peaceful, as if he were asleep. I am sure there was no pain."

"And her . . . my . . . mother?" The words were hard to say, as if she had never learned them until just now.

"Liz lived for a few hours. I brought her here and made her as comfortable as I could. Before she died she gave me a

79

solemn charge. She said, 'I appoint you to be the Guardian of Olwen. That must come first, above all other considerations. Do whatever you must to keep her safe and happy.'" Guardian paused and shifted his weight from one foot to the other. "I have always tried to do that. Until Pegasus Two landed I believed that I had succeeded."

"You had. Oh, you *have*. Dear Guardian, you have been kindness itself. I have had a wonderful life; you must know that. When they came everything changed, but that had nothing to do with you. It certainly wasn't your fault. You couldn't stop me from falling in love with Mark . . . though I think you tried, didn't you? Only I couldn't listen. And it wasn't your fault that Mark fell from the mesa, or that the settlers killed Hobbit. It all just . . . happened."

The room was full of a heavy silence. Olwen turned round in her chair and looked up at Guardian standing just behind her.

"Guardian?"

His face was as impassive as ever, but she knew his moods by now, and she could feel guilt and depression. "Guardian, there's something more, isn't there? What have you done? Did you talk to Mark about me? Is that it? He doesn't want to see me? Did you put him off me in some way? That's not fair. It's . . ."

"Olwen, no. I did nothing like that, I promise. I . . . what I did . . . please listen to me and try to understand why I did it. Your parents died seven years ago—thirteen Earth-years. They had been Keepers of the Isis Light for six Earth-years, and their term of duty was for twenty-five Earth-years, unless a colony ship were to come to Isis before that time. Liz had entrusted you to me. I was your Guardian. I had no choice but to do as she had commanded . . . to keep you safe and happy. I had to consider the possibility of your being marooned here for nineteen more Earth-years, until the relief ship came to take you home to Earth, if you should have wished to go. I asked myself if you could have been happy imprisoned in this valley for all those years, growing up afraid of the ultra-violet and the anoxia of the mountains, never to be really free, as I am free. I knew the kind of woman Liz Pendennis would have liked you to be, a person

without fear or resentment, a person who was free. And it
did work. I feel I was justified. Until Pegasus Two arrived
you were free, you were happy, you were safe."

"Yes, Guardian dear. That is all perfectly true. But what
are you talking about? What do you mean—justified? You
were justified in doing *what*?"

Again the silence hung heavily in the room. Olwen
shivered. Then Guardian spoke. "I changed you. At first I
took away your memory, so that you would not grieve for
the loss of your parents. Then, little by little, surgically and
genetically, I changed you."

"Changed . . . ?"

"Humans are so frail, so poorly adapted." Guardian's
voice was almost angry. "There were a thousand things on
Isis that could have killed you when you were a child, too
small to understand the dangers. I could not guard you every
second. I had my duties to the Light. And you could not
have been happy as a prisoner, I was sure of that. So I
adapted you to Isis. I thickened your skin so that it would be
opaque to the ultra-violet. I gave you an extra eye-lid to
protect your eyes—Ra is so much brighter than Earth's sun."

Olwen's hands crept up to her face. Guardian went on. "I
deepened your rib-cage and extended your vascular system,
much in the way that the deep-sea mammals adapted theirs,
so that you could store much more oxygen at each breath. I
widened your nostrils too, to help you breathe more fully."

"Anything else?"

"I strengthened your ankles and thickened your fingernails
to help you climb. And I changed your metabolism slightly
. . . that shows in your altered skin colour."

"Why?"

"So that the poisonous plants and insects of Isis could not
harm you."

"You did all that for *me*?"

"And for your mother. It was her command."

"She must have loved me very much, to be thinking only
of me when she was dying."

"Oh, she did, Olwen. And so did your father."

"And you, Guardian . . . do you love me?"

"I . . . you . . . you are my reason", he stammered. "You

81

are not angry with me?"

"Why should I be angry? You gave me freedom. You gave me happiness. You gave me Isis. I love you for it, Guardian."

"Thank you." He bowed his head slightly, and for a second seemed almost overcome.

"What I don't understand is that you should feel guilty for what you did for me," Olwen said at last.

"What I did . . ." He stopped and then began again. "You have to understand something difficult. What I did has made you very different from other Earth-type people . . . different from all the settlers . . . different from Mark."

"I know. I've already noticed. I'm better. I'm not confined to UVO suits and oxygen masks. And I am strong. Much stronger than Mark. Guardian!" She stared at him. "Is that why you made me that ridiculous suit and mask? It had nothing to do with viruses—Dr MacDonald was right about that—you were hiding me from the settlers. You didn't want them to see me. Why?"

"I had a plan. I had hoped that you would all get to know each other slowly. That you would learn first to trust, to become friends. Then I hoped that the differences between you would no longer be so important."

"But they're not . . . not to *me*!" Olwen drew in a sharp breath and looked down at her own hands. They were what they had always been, familiar, comfortable extensions of herself. Was there anything wrong with her hands? "Guardian, is that why there are no mirrors? Were you afraid that I couldn't even bear to look at myself. Am I . . . horrible?"

"No, no. It is nothing like that. Oh dear, perhaps that was another wrong decision. It is so difficult to guage a person's emotional reactions, even a person whom I know as well as I know you. But I thought that if you were as familiar with your own appearance as having a mirrored companion might make you, that then *you* might be afraid of the settlers, since you would perceive how different they are from you."

"Am I . . . am I very different?"

"Yes."

"Am I ugly?"

"No! You are not ugly at all. Form and function should be

as one. You function perfectly. You are beautiful."

Olwen stood up. "My head is spinning. It is too much all at once. Mark. Hobbit. And now a mother, a father, a past and a new body . . . I think I must be by myself for a while. Will you do something for me right away?"

"Of course."

"Make a mirror for my room. A big one, please, so that I can see all of myself at once. And can you make it so that I can see the different sides of myself? Can you do that?"

"I will see to it right away. You understand, I did not want you to have a mirror before, but now that you know about yourself . . ."

She nodded. "I'll be on the terrace." She walked out of the cold, strangely inhuman room where Guardian spent so much of his time and into the living room. The scent of cactus flower still lingered in the air, although it was many hours since she had thrown the golden flower into the incinerator. When she walked out onto the terrace the scent became even more powerful, and she realised that it was being wafted to her on the evening breeze from the eastern mountain. The whole upper slope, above the grassline, was a mass of blooming cactus.

She could no more rid Isis of the scent than she could rid herself of her feelings towards Mark. Unless she made Guardian fire the whole mountain-side and destroy the flowers. He would do it if she were to ask him. He would take away the memory of her love for Mark, too, if she were to ask it of him.

She walked to the edge of the terrace and looked across the river valley. To do violence to the mountains and the creatures that lived there, just because she could not bear the scent of the cactus flower, would be hideously wrong. To do violence to her mind, so as to forget her unhappiness, would be equally wrong.

Something strange was beginning to happen inside her. Little memories were swelling up inside her mind and bursting into tiny disassociated glimpses of reality. There were warm hands, strong and gentle, and the feeling of someone tickling her chest with a bearded chin, and the sound of laughter. Her laughter.

She began to understand why Hobbit had meant so much to her. Hobbit was warm, alive, huggable. And that was necessary . . . or had been necessary. She had the painful feeling that she was growing inside so fast that she was going to split and shed her skin, the way a snake does. She could remember laughter . . . Guardian had been so good to her, he had been everything to her. Only Guardian never laughed.

She shut her eyes, the better to endure the waves of emotion that shook her. The only other reality was the rough stone of the balustrade under the grip of her fingers. She was still standing there under the starlight when Guardian came out to tell her that the mirror had been installed in her room. She bent her head in acknowledgement and walked swiftly past him, wrapped in her own thoughts. Guardian's eyes followed her with an expression that on anyone else might have been mistaken for sorrow or regret.

As soon as Olwen entered her room, sweeping aside the curtain that covered the door arch, she saw the Other standing, one arm holding the window curtain, about to move towards her. She stopped abruptly, her heart jolting, suddenly angry. *Nobody* came here. This was her own most private place.

"Who are you?" she snapped, and it seemed that the Other's lips moved mockingly. She walked forward, letting the door curtain fall behind her. Across the wide carpet the Other came to meet her.

Halfway across the room she understood. This was a mirror! The Other, the intruder, was herself. She walked towards herself and touched the surface of the mirror. It was cold and hard; and behind her she could see the whole room crowded into its flatness. As her finger reached out, so did the Other's finger, and, at the cold surface of the glass, they touched.

Olwen had always imagined that a mirror would reflect the same kind of faulty image that she had seen when she had squatted by a rain puddle when she was small, or looked at her fat upside-down face in the bowl of a polished spoon. But this was quite different. This was almost as alive as she was.

She stared at herself, pushing her red hair away from her

face. She had nice bones, she decided, a bit lumpy above the eyes to protect her from the sun, with wide nostrils and a big rib-cage to make the most use of the thin air. She was much more serviceable than the narrow-chested, pinch-faced people from Earth.

Remembering Mark's freckles and the flushed peeling skin that she had noticed on the fairer settlers, she peered at her own skin, and then slipped out of her dressing gown so that she could see all of herself. Her body was strong and smooth, with no freckles or raw places or other deformities, but a nice bronzy green all over. She knew its colour—after all she could see bits of herself every time she stripped—but she had not realised what a striking contrast the bronze made to her red hair. She turned and pirouetted in front of the mirror so that her hair swirled out in a cloud around her.

A tiny reflection from the bedside lamp caught in the glass and shone directly into her eyes, and at once, without her conscious will, a nictating membrane slid over her blue eyes, like a gauze blind. She moved, so that the light no longer shone directly into her eyes, and at once it quickly slid out of sight behind her lower eye-lid. Neat, she thought, and moved so that it happened again.

Olwen turned the side panels of the mirror so that she could see every scrap of herself, and finally she dressed and went back to the living room. Guardian was standing by the fireplace. He looked as if he had not moved since she had left him. All these years he's served me, she thought, planned and schemed to make my life good and happy, and never once has he asked for anything in return. On a sudden wave of gratitude she ran across the room and caught his arms. "Dear Guardian, thank you for my body. It's beautiful!"

He looked down at her, his face expressionless. "You are not angry at what I did?"

"Angry? Why should I be angry? You kept me safe. You gave me a better life than these colonists will ever know. You gave me Isis—the mountains as well as the valleys. I love you for it, Guardian . . . thank you."

"Captain Tryon and Doctor MacDonald are angry with me. They feel that I had no right to change you—that I should have left you as you were."

"All pink and white and soft?" Olwen laughed. "Like a fledgling straight out of the shell! How could I have survived? Never to know the mountains of Isis? Forget about them, Guardian. Surely you don't mind what they say? Is it important to you?"

"Not any more, Olwen. I am yours, and if you are happy then I am happy also."

"Good. Then that's all right. There's only one thing . . . I can't understand, if you've explained it to them properly, why the Captain and the Doctor weren't pleased with what you did. Wouldn't they like to have their poor bodies changed into something as nice and useful as mine? And *all* the settlers . . . you could make them like me, too. Then they can share all Isis, and not just the stuffy valley." Then they will all look like me, she thought. Mark will be like me . . .

Guardian was silent for a long time. When he spoke it was slowly as if he was choosing his words. "You were still very young when I began to change you. Only four Earth years old. Most of what I did was genetic manipulation. I gave your skin new messages that it would always remember. I made it thick and scaly, to protect you from ultra-violet and from thorn-bushes. I told your bones to grow sturdier, so that you would be safe in the mountains. Because you were so young it was possible.

"The settlers are different. Even the youngest is nine Earth-years old. It's too late. My techniques would not work. I could only make surgical changes. It would be slow and painful, and underneath the changes the old Earth-type body would be always trying to break through. When the skin renewed itself it would be the old useless Earth skin again." His voice faded. "Olwen, I'm sorry."

"I see." She walked slowly to the window that gave a glimpse of the new village far below to the right, its lights a tiny swarm of fire-flies. "The suit you made for me, all smooth and pink and white . . . how long did you expect me to go on wearing it? How long did you expect to be able to keep up the deception that I was just like them?"

"Not for long, Olwen. Just until they got to know you."

"The pink and white me? What was the *use*, Guardian? Didn't you realise that knowing that mask was not knowing *me* at all?" She laughed, a short bitter sound that made him move towards her. "You're too good at everything you do, that's the trouble. Too clever by half!"

"What do you mean?"

"Why didn't you make that mask ordinary, even a little ugly? Why did you have to fashion it with just the kind of prettiness that would make Mark fall in love with it?"

"I am so sorry. It is just that I think that you are so very beautiful, so when I made the mask I tried to translate that beauty into their terms."

"Into *their* terms," Olwen repeated the words. "And then . . ." She turned suddenly, her hands to her mouth. "I must be very stupid. *Now* I understand what happened when Mark climbed to the mesa top and found me there. I was alone. I was . . . myself." She gestured to her face and body. "He saw me the way I really am. He cried out. I saw the horror in his face as I turned. I thought it was because he was slipping, because he knew he was going over the edge. But it wasn't that at all, was it? It didn't happen that way at all. First ᵗhe horror. The cry. *Then* the step backwards. Oh, Guardian, he saw me as I am and he was disgusted!"

"You are mistaken, Olwen. He slipped. He should never have tried to tackle the mesa alone."

"Guardian, dear, you are a quite dreadful liar! And what about today? What about the hunters? One of them was going to kill me, you know. Just like that . . . would you believe it? He pointed his gun at me, but the other one took it away from him. And what about the people in the village? They screamed and ran and hid. Guardian, you've given me a beautiful body, and they all *hate* it."

"It is not that. They were surprised, that is all. And guilty. They had killed your friend Hobbit. And you the Keeper of the Light! And after all, you *were* very angry."

"I must learn to hide my feelings then. My feelings and my face." She spoke bitterly and Guardian moved quickly towards her.

"Olwen, don't!"

"Don't what?"

"Don't change. Don't become . . . less beautiful."

"I must. I was a child until now. I didn't understand how

things would be. I know now. An adult has to armour himself, put up defences so as not to get hurt . . ."

"No!"

"*You* say that? Aren't you armoured, Guardian? You always protect yourself from too many questions, from too much closeness. Oh, I understand. It's you . . . just the way you're made. But why would you tell me to be any different? Why should I leave myself open to hate and fear and . . . and disgust?" Olwen's voice trembled and she swallowed and clenched her hands. After a while she was able to go on, her voice as level and emotionless as Guardian's. "I will never wear that mask and suit again. Please destroy them. I will never go down into the village, nor have anything to do with the settlers again. I will forget them. We will go on just as we did before they came."

"You know that is not possible."

"I don't see why not. We were perfectly happy before the Pegasus landed, just the two of us." She stuck her chin up and stared blankly down at the village. The lights shimmered diamond-pointed through her tears.

"But they *have* landed. Your job as Keeper of the Isis Light has changed. You have a vital role to play as advisor to the new colony. You must sit on their councils, make sure that they make no plans dangerous to their own future. You must . . ."

"No!" She turned from the window, her eyes huge with unshed tears. "You can do all that, far better than I. I am not really the Keeper of the Light. You are. You kept it faithfully all the years that I was busy growing up and learning. *You* go to their councils."

"Olwen, I am nothing to them. They will not listen to me."

That shocked her almost more than anything else that had happened. "What do you mean? You are *Guardian*."

He shrugged. "Nevertheless. You may call it prejudice. But I tell you, they will not listen to me."

"Very well. I will compromise. You will attend the councils as my delegate. And if the council needs my advice on anything they may climb up here and get it. For I will never go down into that valley again, I swear it!"

Chapter Eight

Olwen kept her word. For the next few turns of Shu and Nut she either stayed in the house or roamed the slopes of the mountains above the Cascades. She could not bear to go back to the top of the mesa, and even her other favourite places had lost their savour. By the time the little moons had raced across the sky a dozen times and fast-moving Shu had caught up with Nut again, she was cross and restless, and for the first time in her life she felt like a prisoner.

"I've got to get away," she told Guardian, when he found her packing a sleeping robe and a change of clothing. "I've got to be by myself. To think and be alone. I won't be gone longer than a week."

"At least tell me where you are going," Guardian begged.

"North," she said vaguely. "I don't know. If it'll make you happy I'll take a transponder so you'll know where I am. But please leave me alone, just for a week."

"You are sure you will be all right?" His voice was almost humble.

"Of course I will. You made me for Isis, remember?"

After she had left the house Olwen wished she had not allowed her bitterness to show so clearly. Almost she went back to say she was sorry. But Guardian was no longer in the living room. Perhaps he had not heard her, she told herself, as she dumped her few pieces of gear into the floater and headed north.

She followed the course of the river towards its far mountain source, and in a wide, long valley came upon unknown territory. Where the ground dropped away she parked the floater on a southern slope to recharge its power cells, slung her bed-roll over her shoulder, and set out on foot.

It was late spring, and in these temperate latitudes of Isis the days were hot and dry and only at night did it cool down. She kept to the high country, striding through Alpine meadows of short blue turf in which hid a hundred varieties of minute flowers. There was a bee-like creature which made its home in the fissures of rocks and gathered the nectar busily, so that she walked to a background music of drowsy humming. Once she came upon one of their nests, hanging against a cliff, and she broke off a pinnacle of brown honeycomb to add to her food supplies. The bees complained angrily at her intrusion and tried to sting her, but she brushed them off her skin and walked on.

On the third day she found a new valley, with a river in it that flowed northward, the opposite way to the river back home. It was a high valley, with the air still thin and clean, not like the moist heaviness of the settlers' valley, and she found it a pleasant place to linger. After she had filled her water bottle she bathed and then lay drowsily in the sun to dry herself off.

Close by, on the slope above her, was a grove of the bamboo-like grasses of which Guardian had built much of their furniture. This was an old grove, older than any she had seen before, with great stalks that rose far above her head. The leaves rippled like silver banners in the gentle wind that sighed up the valley from the north, and the hollow stalks knocked against each other as the wind moved them to and fro, and made a solemn music.

Supper that evening was fish, fresh-caught in the icy stream and roasted on a stick over the fire. She sat by the embers, eating the delicate shreds of pinkish flesh and watching the glow of a spectacular sunset flame the west almost to the zenith. As the glow died she replenished her fire and sat on, watching the stars come out one by one. Little by little the silence worked its way into her being, and she began to find her way back to the quiet core of herself, the part that she had lost when Pegasus Two had landed.

The peace and beauty of the valley held her to it with a deep attraction and she decided to wander no further. She slept without moving under the quiet stars, and only woke when Ra was on her face. She had planned a lazy day by the river, but after she had eaten a restlessness came over her which drove her to the higher ground above the valley. She walked through the bamboo grove and up through a sloping meadow of waist-high grass heavy with ripening red seed heads, until she came to the short blue turf again and the alpine flowers and the bare red crags above.

Still something drove her on, and she began to climb the side of a great twin-peaked mountain. By lunch-time she had reached the northern face and crouched down on a relatively wide ledge to eat cold fish and bread and honey. The river, like a silver eel, wriggled north across a wide plain, losing itself in a lavender haze below the far mountains.

Haze? She gasped and thanked whatever instinct had driven her up to the heights. That was not haze. It was sand. A tremendous wind was tearing across the plain from the northern mountains, sucking up sand and dust in whirling pillars of red and purple.

Within a few minutes the entire valley below her had been blotted out, and even up on the heights she could feel particles of sand grit against her teeth and sting her eyes. She worked her way around the moutain face until she found a deep crevice, almost a cave, opening to the west, sheltered from the worst of the wind. Here she squatted in the warm midday dusk to wait out the storm.

Ra no longer shone blue-white, but glowed sullenly, like a hot coal. Then even that dimmed and she could not see its light at all. The wind screamed and shook the roots of the mountain. Had there ever been a storm like this one? Was this storm like the one that had killed her mother and father? Snug in her cave she wondered how the settlers would be making out in their fragile plastic houses. Would they be safe? Would they know what to do? And would they have the sense to ask Guardian?

A scuffling and whimpering outside broke her train of thought. What could it be, loud enough to hear above the wind? She wrapped her scarf around her mouth and nose and peered out into the purple fog. There, just below her on the slope, was one of Hobbit's brothers, just a baby really, struggling desperately up the steep rock towards the cave. She whistled through her teeth to it and hauled, with a care for its

91

spines. A scrabble and a heave, and it was safe inside, shaking itself vigorously, so that the air was full of sand and dust and Olwen began to sneeze. She washed the creature's eyes with some of her precious water, and poured a little into a hollow of the floor for it to drink. Then it put its huge clawed paws across her knees and they sat in companionable silence to watch the storm rage.

All through the long afternoon the wind shook the mountain, and it was not until shortly before sunset that it abruptly died down, and the sand began to drift down into the valley below them. Ra glowed with a fiery glare and the entire sky was bathed in crimson light, as if reflecting the red dust that lay thickly all over the land.

Even when the last traces of sun had vanished from the sky Olwen had no desire to sleep. This was a day of unusual wonders and she did not want it to end. Across her knees the little Hobbit snored softly. Though he was only a pup he must have weighed a hundred kilos, but she had not the heart to shift him. As if she were keeping vigil, she watched over Isis throughout the night.

After midnight the aurora, like a false dawn, began to fill the northern sky with cold green light. It grew and strengthened from flimsy curtains swaying in the cosmic wind to great cathedral pillars and arches carved from translucent jade, shot through with veins of marvellous rosy pink. She could hear the faint crackling music of it, like singing ice, and her red hair stirred in the heavily charged atmosphere.

She wondered again about the settlers. Would they remember the significance of the wind storm, the sunset and the aurora? Would they feel, as she could feel right now, that in the peace and stillness of the night an even more deadly storm was raging over Isis? Would they understand the explosive burst of energy from Ra that had sent a stream of cosmic rays spewing across the surface of Isis?

Olwen forgot her anger towards the settlers. She thought of the Captain, the doctor, of the child with the negroid features who had played so unconcernedly as she had stormed down the village street. She thought of Mark. God, keep them safe, she prayed. Let them listen to Guardian. Make them do what he says. Her arms tightened around the little

92

Hobbit, so that it grunted in its sleep and twitched its hairy barbed tail.

She finally fell asleep towards dawn, and when she woke again it was already noon. Her instinct told her that it would be safe to move, and she was *starving*. By the time she had clambered down to the valley again, little Hobbit bounding along beside her, the water in the river had begun to flow clear again, though red dust still thickly coated the smooth shore stones and lay, like a pinkish bloom, over the silver leaves of the bamboo grove.

She caught enough fish for both of them. The little Hobbit was perfectly capable of catching its own dinner, of course, but it gave them both great pleasure for her to feed it, and for it to accept the gift.

Olwen spent the rest of the day close to the river. There was a small cataract where the water spilled down from the mountains above the grove. It was no more than three metres high, but the water moved fast. Under its icy torrent she washed the dust from her hair, and changed and washed her clothes. Then she wandered among the meadow grass, shaking enough pollen from them to make cakes, mixed with the wild honey and baked on a hot stone close to the fire. She found spring stone-berries on the slope that was watered with spray from the cataract, and with fish and the honey-cakes she and little Hobbit shared their supper.

She went to bed early, wrapped up in her sleeping robe, with little Hobbit hunched up at her back, a wonderful draught excluder. She woke up, refreshed and at peace, in the jade-green dawn, and lay and listened to the treble sound of the water and the deep bass notes of the bamboo stems softly booming as they touched each other, while far over her head a lark sang.

"I would like to stay here for ever" she told little Hobbit. But as she said it she realised that she had already been gone for four nights and should spend no more than one day here before returning home.

Once she realised that, the day turned into a busyness of organizing enough food for the walk back to the floater. She caught and filleted several flat-fish and lay them on hot rocks in the sun to dry. Then she found a bush full of last year's winterberries. They were dry and sweet and good to chew on the march. By the time she had picked enough of them it was time to make supper, and the last precious day was almost gone.

She woke, in the pre-dawn light. Hobbit was still snoring peacefully beside her, and she packed up her gear quietly and set off south up the river valley towards the high saddle of the watershed without waking him. She did not stop for breakfast and she did not look back until her valley was almost out of sight.

Then, at the top of the ridge that would hide it from her, she looked back. Bamboo Valley lay below her in bands of iridescent colour; the short blue upland turf, the delicately nodding plumes of red-grass, the silvery whisper of the bamboo grove. The river, like a line of molten silver, poured down the rocks and wriggled across the great plain to the far range, the mountains where she had never been, the mountains that faced the sea.

A sudden agitation in the long red-grass brought her eyes back to the foreground. Bother! There was little Hobbit bounding towards her with that same joyful trusting expression that her own Hobbit had had. If only he had gone on sleeping until she was out of sight.

She knelt down and put her arms around his neck and hugged him. "You can't come with me," she told him. "They'll only kill you, the way they killed my Hobbit. They don't understand, you see. They think that because you're ugly you must be dangerous. They're afraid of you." Her tears stained his neck-fur dark, and he turned his head and licked her face. She pushed him away, her strength against his hundred-kilo bulk, and at last he seemed to understand that it was not just another game. He sat down on his long bony haunches, his tongue dropping past his dagger-like canines. "I *will* be back," she promised. "I *will* see you again."

She turned her back on the rainbow colours of the valley. She left her newfound friend, and toiled up over the saddle. All the joy seemed to have been bled out of the day, and even though the sky was cloudless Ra did not seem as warm as usual, nor the mountain air as tingling.

She walked fast, paying little heed to the folding ranges she clambered up and down, and in two days she was back at the place where she had left the floater. She was flat and tired and longing for a shower. But there was no peace when she reached home. Guardian was in a turmoil.

"But I promised you that I would be back within a week, and here I am. The seventh day and it's not evening yet."

"I feared for you in the storm."

"I was safe enough, snugly tucked away in a cave, above the dust and out of the wind."

"Dust . . . wind . . . Olwen, the solar outburst emitted the greatest radiation since the storm that killed your parents. If I had known it was coming I would never have let you go. I must test you to make sure that you have not been damaged by radiation."

"I thought this skin of mine was designed to be proof against anything Ra could throw at it."

"Yes, well, perhaps. But this storm was *very* bad."

Olwen submitted to Guardian's battery of tests, her mind far away in the enchanted high valley full of the music of the bamboo and the whisper of the deep red-grass, and it was not until he had finished and pronounced her in perfect health that she remembered the settlers again.

"Were they all right? Where did they shelter? Those houses would be no good." She did not ask after Mark. She could not say his name, though when she thought about him she felt as if her heart was being squeezed by a slow painful giant hand.

"I advised them to shelter in Pegasus Two. The ship is, of course, designed to withstand the hard radiation of space. But by the time it was safe for them to emerge they had become very uncomfortable. I gather that it was hot and stuffy and they became uneasy. They must have caves, like these. The Captain is coming to talk to you about it this evening."

"Here? So soon? Guardian, I've just got back."

"You are the Keeper of the Light, by inheritance if not by choice, Olwen. I am only your servant and the settlers know it. They prefer not to listen to me."

"Lucky for them that they did! How dare they call you a servant. You are my friend, a thousand times friend. Don't they understand that you are much much wiser than I am? That you know so much more?"

Guardian bowed his head slightly in acknowledgement of her outburst. "Nevertheless, it is you who are the Keeper, and it is you whom the Captain wishes to see. If you feel too tired I will postpone the meeting until tomorrow morning, but it should be no later than that."

Olwen sighed. She could feel her new-won peace shredding away from her in tatters. "I'll see him tonight. After dinner."

She showered and washed her hair, and then dressed with particular care in a sheath of red-gold stuff cunningly shaped from minute overlapping scales. Her hair, brushed into a crackling nimbus, was just a shade more red than the dress, and her face and bare arms and shoulders looked greenly iridescent.

Captain Jonas Tryon, climbing laboriously up the steep stone "staircase" to the terrace of the house, saw her first bathed in the lights of the living room, and thought she looked like an exotic and intelligent lizard. He shook hands, momentarily taken aback that her palm should be as warm and moist as his. Subconsciously he had been expecting the cold dryness of a reptile.

Throughout the evening's conversation the same problem recurred. Whenever he thought of her as the Keeper of the Isis Light, a native of a distant planet, then he could see how beautiful she was. There was a dignified symmetry in the wide nose and heavy eyebrows that balanced the weight of glorious red hair cascading down her shoulders. The goldish-green of her skin was exotic, and even the nictating membrane, which he saw slide across her eyes in a sudden light reflection, had a strange kind of fascination.

But when he saw her as Olwen Pendennis, the daughter of his old friend Gareth . . . and, oh, how the colour of her hair tore at past memories . . . then she was disgusting. Words like Neanderthal and reptilean sprang to his mind. He thought of Dr Jekyll and Mr Hyde; and the horrifying monster movies of his childhood crowded

96

unbidden into his mind.

Now, at last, the puzzle of Mark's fall and subsequent behaviour was crystal clear. Mark had said nothing—nothing that made any sense. When he had regained consciousness and recovered from the pain-killers that had kept him dopey for the first day he had only stared and shuddered and could say nothing that made any sense. Only when they had asked him if he wished Olwen to come and see him had he reacted, in hysterical panic. . .

She was talking, and he had not heard a word. The Captain pulled himself together and tried to pay attention to what she—what Olwen Pendennis—was saying. Her words were startlingly conventional, like any hostess back on Earth.

"It is cool on the terrace. But if you would feel more comfortable we can go inside."

He stared and then shook his head confusedly. "It doesn't matter. The terrace will do very well."

She showed him a seat, and curled up gracefully on a couch at right angles to his chair. "Guardian will bring us drinks," she told him tranquilly.

"Why do you call him that?" The personal quality of the name irritated him, he couldn't have said why.

"My mother appointed him as my Guardian when she was dying. He has done everything for me. He has fed me, clothed me, protected me, educated me. Loved me. He is the wisest person on Isis." Her strange eyes challenged him to contradict her.

"I'm sure you are right," he said pacifically, and covered up the insincerity he was sure she must have felt by looking around . . . Really, this was the most attractive place, a little like an incredibly expensive hotel on the French Riviera which he had once visited, when he was younger and more reckless, and a new captain's pay had seemed like a fortune. "This is very beautiful."

She inclined her head slightly. Could she smile? The look in her eyes was quite disconcerting. He had never seen her smile. Could reptiles smile?

"I will show you over the house when we have had our drinks, if you wish."

As if on cue Guardian, as she called him—ridiculous

name—walked soft-footedly out of the shadows and put a tray down on the table between them. He offered a delicate stemmed glass to the Captain. "The juice of a local fruit, sir. I believe you will enjoy it."

He moved silently away, the perfect servant expressed in every movement of his body. Jonas Tryon wondered suddenly if he were playing the part. Really, it was almost *too* perfect. He turned in time to see the Keeper's lips part, as if she had wanted to call him back. He saw her fingers tighten on the stem of her glass . . . good God, those fingers were like claws . . . and then her eyelids lowered and her figure relaxed into stillness. She drooped silently over her drink.

The Captain removed his oxygen mask and sipped his drink cautiously. It was cold, a little acid, with a clean refreshing after-taste that magically relieved the exhaustion of a hot hard day's work. He drank more deeply and then firmly put the glass down on the table. He saw her make a small defensive movement. She was quick. For a second he wondered if she was telepathic, but then he dismissed the idea as ridiculous. She could hardly have sat so calmly, so perfectly the gracious hostess, if she had been able to listen in on his thoughts about her.

He took a deep breath of oxygen. "I am concerned about that solar storm," he said briskly. "The data you have been sending back to Earth in recent years did not lead us to expect anything as severe."

She shrugged. "I myself remember no storms as bad as that," she admitted.

"Then what do you think? Is this a trend? When will it happen again? What are we to expect?"

"You must ask Guardian. The material is in the data banks. Guardian can give you a statistical analysis of it. You have only to ask."

"I would rather have your opinion. What did you feel about the last storm?"

She shrugged again, and he watched in half fascination, half horror, how her hair slid back, exposing more of her greenish-bronze shoulder. "I was not here. I was up among the northern mountains when the storm hit. Perhaps it was worse here."

"You were out there? In the storm? Alone?"

"Why not? Isis is my home." She made an unexpectedly beautiful gesture that embraced the valley, the darkening mountains, the sky.

"Yes, but . . . where did you find shelter?"

"In a crevice on the mountain, a cave almost. It faced west and was deep enough to keep out the wind and most of the dust."

"But what about the radiation?"

"That does not bother me."

"You're joking, of course. Please don't. This is important. We are talking about the safety of my passengers."

"I don't joke. Not with you, Captain." She looked straight at him, and Jonas Tryon realised with a shock that to her he was the enemy. He had been so busy analysing his own feelings about the Keeper that he had not even considered what she might be thinking about him. He saw it in her eyes now. Intruder. Disrupter.

But her voice was mild enough as she went on, "Guardian has already explained to you that when he was left in charge of me, just a toddler, he could not make all Isis safe for me, so he made me safe for Isis."

The Captain found himself stammering. This was an area where he had rather not tread. "I know. Yes, he did explain. But . . . but, well, *hard* radiation?"

"Nevertheless." She spread out her hands, and then fell silent, holding her misty glass and looking out abstractedly into the firefly-filled night. Her attitude told him unmistakeably that she wished that he would go away. The Captain found himself floundering, feeling suddenly boorish and ill at ease.

He tried to pull himself together. "I need your help," he blurted out.

She turned to look directly at him, her strange eyes beautifully luminous. She did not speak.

"The settlers *must* have a better warning system. There was barely time to get everyone under cover. As they spread out, move away from the village, get more land under cultivation, perhaps explore beyond this valley, it'll be even more difficult. Your . . . Guardian warned us as soon as he suspected

99

the oncoming storm. You were closer to it. Did he give you plenty of warning?"

She stared and then shook her head. "No. I was alone. Out of touch. I wanted it so."

"Then how did you know?"

"Oh!" She put down her drink abruptly and looked at her claws—no, hands, damn it—as if she were trying to relive the moments. Then she shook her head slowly. "I was down in the valley. I don't exactly know what happened. I was restless. Something made me climb the mountain that morning. I don't know what or why. And I saw the storm far off, in the north."

Jonas Tryon sighed. It had been a hard four days. "That's not very scientific, Miss Pendennis. Perhaps you could think about it some more. There must have been some kind of sign, something that you were aware of without knowing it . . . after a lifetime here you are obviously more weather-wise. Do you understand what I mean?"

She nodded. "But I don't think there is anything that'll help. I don't remember being aware of a storm coming on previous occasions. But of course Guardian was always there to warn me to come home in plenty of time."

"Which brings me to my second point. Shelter. We must make cosmic storm shelters in the mesa."

Olwen opened her mouth to protest, but Captain Tryon lifted his hand in a silencing gesture. "We won't intrude on your privacy. We will make them right at the bottom of the cliff, where we can be comfortable without oxygen. Believe me, we have *no* interest in upper Isis. We will start lasering out shelters immediately."

"You are telling me this? You are not asking it?"

"Yes. This is not your planet exclusively any more, Miss Pendennis. Your parents were employed by Stellar Transport. STC owns this planet. You do not. Pegasus Two is one of their ships and I am one of their captains. *I* am in charge of Isis now."

The colour slowly drained from her face. It was extraordinary to watch. It was as if the gold faded away, leaving only a sickly green. She leapt to her feet. Her glass toppled over, rolled to the edge of the table and smashed on the stone floor.

She did not seem to be aware of it. He saw her hands clench. "And did *that* give you the right to have Hobbit killed?" she screamed at him.

"Hobbit?" He was totally at a loss, and wondered, for one heart-stopping instant, if she were mad. Those claws could make mincemeat of a person, and he was not armed . . . "Won't you sit down and tell me what it is you're talking about?" he asked soothingly, trying to keep his voice firm and commanding.

"No, I will not. And I will remind you that though you may be in charge of Isis, this is still *my* home." She walked swiftly away from him along the length of the terrace, the train of her gold-scale dress making a small whispery sound on the stone.

"I'm sorry," he called. He did not dare follow her in case she were to turn on him. "Really, I don't understand. Who is Hobbit?"

"My friend. He was my friend." She turned, came back and sat down suddenly on the edge of a chair. He could see in the light from inside the house that her eyes were filled with tears. While one part of his mind felt compassion and a twinge of guilt the other, scientific part, noticed that the girl could cry. Like a human. Unlike a reptile.

"When? Where? What happened?" He urged her to go on.

"You don't *know*? And you're in *charge*?" Her voice was scornful, and idiotically he found himself flushing. "It was down in the grasslands," she went on. "Two of your men shot Hobbit."

Captain Tryon shook his head. If he was ever to win her co-operation he must rid her of this delusion. "All we have killed is some deer-like creatures. We do eat meat, you know, especially when we are working so hard. We were told that the game on Isis is plentiful . . . it was in your reports. That is all, I swear. Except . . ." He stopped.

"Except for Hobbit." Her voice was flat.

"There was a terrifying beast, like a . . . oh, it defied description . . . like a hairy dragon. We were told that they inhabited only the uplands of Isis."

"That was Hobbit."

"He attacked a party of surveyors."

"Either you are lying, Captain Tryon, or they are. He borrowed one of their striped sticks. It was only to play with. We were playing fetch and carry." Her face suddenly twisted and she hid it in her hands.

"Hobbit?" He found himself asking idiotically. "Why *Hobbit*, for pete's sake!"

"Why not? He was mine. Guardian found him alone and gave him to me when he was only a pup. So I called him Hobbit. I got the name out of an old book."

"But those teeth . . . the jaw . . . the size of the beast. The men told me . . . I'd swear they weren't exaggerating."

She stood above him, staring down at his face. He could see where her tears had made shiny trails down her face. "Hobbit was as gentle as a dormouse. *He couldn't help looking the way he did*, you know!" She threw the words at him, like a challenge, like a blow. She kept her eyes on his face, forcing him to look up at her.

"I . . . I am so sorry," he stammered at last, and managed to look away. "It was a mistake . . . you do understand, don't you? A misunderstanding . . ."

She turned away. "Was that all you wished to talk about, Captain? I am a little tired."

"Of course." Captain Tryon moved towards the stairway, thankful that this incredibly difficult interview was finally coming to an end. "Just one more point. The . . . Guardian has said that you will not come to our council meetings. You should be there. We may need your expertise. Won't you reconsider?"

She shook her head. "I will never go down among you Earth people again. Guardian will attend the meetings. His expertise is far greater than mine. And you will honour it." She turned and her eyes flashed so fiercely that he found himself stammering.

"Of course. That is understood. Perhaps you will change your mind later. Believe me, I am sorry. If we had been warned about your pet . . . if you had just let us know. As for the rest . . ." He fumbled for words, while she stared at him stonily. "We shall become accustomed to each other, I am sure. There may be a period of adjustment, but it will work out. Why, all over the galaxy there are species who live

102

in harmony with one another, with Man . . ."

He stopped when he saw the expression on her face and realised what he had said. Her voice dropped like ice into the horrible silence. "I too am a member of your species, Captain, or I was. Perhaps I am not any more. Perhaps you are right in thinking of me as an alien. I know I am different from you. You see—I do not kill."

She swept into the house, leaving the Captain standing alone on the terrace, with the lights glowing softly and the stars blazing in the cold sky above.

Chapter Nine

Three days later a letter came from Mark. It was sealed up inside an envelope, with her name scrawled across the front . . . OLWEN PENDENNIS. She had never received a letter before. She had never seen her name written by anyone other than herself and Guardian. She stood in the middle of the living room, turning it over and over in her hands.

"You open it so, with a knife," Guardian told her and held out a helping hand.

"No. I'll do it. It's my letter." She slit the envelope, pulled out the two sheets of paper it contained and began to read.

Dear Olwen,

The doctor has not allowed me to write and thank you for saving my life, but I can really move my wrist now, so I'm going ahead anyway, and I hope you can understand this scrawl. They told me that you found me and kept my oxygen mask in place until your Guardian could get me down, and that without you I would have died of anoxia even if I hadn't fallen the rest of the way down the mesa. It was a dumb thing for me to do by myself, but I wanted to see you—it was something special, but the silly thing is I can't remember what.

It's awfully hot down here in the middle of the day, especially stuck in bed. I miss our trips. Everyone else is perfectly contented with the valley, but perhaps that's because none of them has seen what it's like on upper Isis.

Olwen caught her breath and turned away from Guardian, who was standing, politely attentive, at her elbow. She could still see, in a ghastly slow-motion unreeling of time, the

104

backwards fall of Mark off the mesa, and the look of horror on his face during that final second. It was as clear as if it had happened only that morning, and yet to Mark it was as if the horror had never happened. She walked slowly out onto the terrace and sat on a shaded couch, hung swing-like from an overhang of rock. After a while she picked up the letter from her lap and went on reading.

As soon as I am fit enough I want to go exploring with you again. Perhaps we could go north, to your beautiful valley . . .

"Guardian!" The anger in her voice surprised her.

"Yes, Olwen?" He appeared so quickly that he must have been waiting for her summons.

"How does Mark know about my valley?"

"Perhaps from the Council . . ."

"You told the Council about *my* valley?"

"Of course. Who knows, your exploration may prove very useful one day."

"But it was *my* place . . . my very own."

"For a while, perhaps. Later the settlers will want to move away, expand across the rest of Isis. And they are restricted to the valleys."

"This one, my one, was so high. There wouldn't be enough oxygen for them, I'm sure," she pleaded.

"That will be for the Council to decide in due course. But why worry? It will not be for years. It may never be. But it had to be reported."

"Everything is being taken from me." Her lips felt stiff and it was hard to say the words properly. "Hobbit. Mark. Isis. Myself."

"No one can take you from yourself. That is impossible."

"Oh no, it isn't. I can feel it happening. Oh, Guardian, I feel so strange. I don't know what they're thinking . . . how can I trust them? You know how horrible they think I am, yet when the Captain was here the other evening he pretended that everything was ordinary. Is Mark doing the same thing in this letter? I don't understand. Is there no one I can trust?"

"You can trust me, now and for ever."

"You told the Council about my valley! Oh, I'm not being

fair—I know you had to do it. How I wish that we were back the way we were before they came. Everything's changing. I'm changing. I've even found myself wondering about you . . ."

"Hush. It will be all right. You must give things time to work out, that's all. What was in the letter Mark sent you?"

"Oh." Olwen lifted the pages again. "I never did finish it."

I wish it were possible to explore without a UVO suit and oxygen. Some day, when there are enough of us on the planet to make it work, we'll get more oxygen into the air, from plants, or maybe from the rocks. Those red and purple mountains must be chock full of oxides, and we'll never run out of solar power to break them down. Then we'll be as free as you are on Isis.

Why don't you visit me? The others won't talk about you. They stare and then change the subject. What's the matter? I heard about your pet being killed. I'm sorry, but you do realise it was just a mistake, don't you? And they say it was the ugliest thing in creation.

Please come and see me. I miss you. I miss the things we talked about, music, books, everything. I miss your beautiful voice and the way you laugh. Maybe this accident was a bit of luck. I'd probably never have got up the nerve to tell you face to face how I feel. But I've had lots of time to work out the right words. Why don't you come? You know there are no viruses down here, that was just a crazy idea of your Guardian. Forget about Hobbit. After all, he's gone now. And he was only an animal. This is us.

I love you,
Mark

She stood up and the pages fluttered to the ground. "I don't understand any of this. Is he pretending that I'm no different? Why? What kind of game is it?"

Guardian picked up the pages, scanned them and folded them neatly. "Sometimes a blow to the head causes loss of memory of the few minutes before the blow. Since he does not seem to remember the actual fall, he may not remember what went before—if indeed anything did. Perhaps you were mistaken. Perhaps it is of no importance to him that you look somewhat different from the other women here. After all, if he truly loves you it should be of no importance at all."

"Oh, how I wish I could believe that! Oh, it's so ironic. He's forgotten that awful day, and I can't forget. Maybe you should hit me on the head!" She laughed bitterly.

"That is an irrational suggestion."

"I know that! Do you always have to be so darn logical?" She sniffed back tears. "Oh, *what* am I going to do?"

"You could visit him as he asks."

"Go down there? I *can't*." Vividly she remembered the expressions on the faces, the last time she had gone to the village, filled with anger at Hobbit's death. Fear. Horror. All except one . . . there had been one child's face that had been different . . .

"You could ignore his letter."

"That way I would never know if he was telling me the truth, if he meant all this."

"Then you could write and tell him why you will not go down and see him."

Olwen paced restlessly up and down the terrace. Then she made up her mind. "I won't pretend," she said firmly. "You must take a photograph of me. A good one, in colour. And I will write a letter to go with it."

It was easy to say, but it took Olwen the rest of the morning and many crumpled sheets of Guardian's best paper before she was at last satisfied. By then the pictures had been taken, enlarged and mounted. She spread them out on the table and hovered over them.

"Do you think this one?"

Guardian nodded. "I think it is the best. You are beautiful."

"Don't give him the picture until he's read my letter," she warned him. "And you will wait, won't you. For . . . for . . ." She stammered and fell silent.

"I will of course wait for a reply," Guardian said matter-of-factly. "Indeed this is the best photograph, Olwen. I think he will be very pleased with it."

"It did turn out well, didn't it? Oh, do you think

· 107

everything is going to be all right?"

"He would be mad not to appreciate you, just as you are, Olwen. Do not worry."

After he had left she changed into a simple jumpsuit and climbed to the top of the mesa. She had not gone back since the day of Mark's fall. She had not seen Hobbit's grave. Guardian had lasered out a hollow in the solid rock, and then covered it with a cairn of stones, so now there were two monuments on the mesa, the Light and the grave.

It was blazingly hot on the flat shadeless top, and all the little burrowing creatures were asleep underground. She felt restless and edgy—the way she had felt that day in Bamboo Valley, when some urge had made her climb the mountain. Another storm? She looked to the north, but the sky was a stainless green-blue without a single wisp of cloud.

She lay in the little patch of shadow under the Light and thought about fate. That Mark should have been born five parsecs away on Earth. That his parents should have been picked as colonists out of the thousands and thousands who applied. That he should be on Isis. Her kind of person. I love you, Olwen, he had written. She lay on her back in the dappled shade and whispered, "I love you too, Mark." It was all so perfect, like the right warp and weft coming together to weave a beautiful enduring fabric. If only . . . Would he still like her? Would her being different matter?

She could not lie still. Ignoring the heat she walked over to the south-eastern edge of the mesa. She could see the village through the mist of atmosphere, though the figures were too tiny and vague to differentiate. They were like fire-beetles, running in and out of the tiny house cocoons. Through her binoculars she could see a group going off into the long grass to hunt, and another going down to the lake to fish. They talked. They were always talking. She could not hear them, but she knew what they were doing by the way they stopped and waved their arms about.

What did they talk about all the time? Was it music and poetry and the ideas that bubble up inside one's mind on hot slow days? Did they talk the way she and Mark had talked? Or were they just filling in the awful empty spaces of a new planet.

108

There was Guardian, unmistakable, stalking tall and straight up the village street towards the Cascades. She left her look-out spot and scrambled down the steep cliff-side to the house. She was on the terrace before him, and she waited impatiently, wishing that it was in Guardian's nature to hurry, when hurrying was so obviously necessary. She could have screamed at the neat deliberation with which he set each foot down on the rock-strewn bank of the river.

Suddenly she felt she could not bear to know what had happened, and she fled through the house to the kitchen and began, distractedly, to make herself a fruit drink. There Guardian found her. He said nothing, and his face gave nothing away. He held out a single folded sheet of paper. Olwen put her drink down with a jolt that splashed it all over the counter.

She left Guardian to mop up the spill and walked swiftly away from him, down the length of the living room, holding the note between her two hands. To open it was impossible. Not to open it was unbearable. She took a deep breath and forced her fingers to unfold the paper and her eyes to read it.

Mark's writing was large and forceful, and he had used a black stylo, but Olwen had to blink and refocus her eyes before she could make sense out of the two lines of writing that were all the note contained.

I will abide by your decision. I wish things had been different. Mark.

Two lines. Only two lines, and they said nothing at all. Had she made a decision? She didn't think so. All the carefully worded, crumpled and discarded drafts of the letter she had written to him went through her mind. Decision? Surely in the end she had done nothing more than tell the whole truth about herself and leave the rest up to him.

. . . 'I wish things had been different' . . . What things? Did he mean his feelings? Her feelings? Convention? And at the end . . . 'Mark'. Not . . . 'love, Mark.' Just 'Mark'. Really, that word was the only thing in the letter that said anything at all. The rest was all evasion. Unless perhaps he had not written 'love' even though he had wanted to, out of a sense of delicacy towards her supposed feelings. Maybe he had *felt* 'love', even though he hadn't written it.

109

"Guardian!" she called, and he was there, quietly attentive, as if he had been doing nothing at all but wait for her call. "Guardian, when Mark read my letter, did he say anything? How did he look?"

"After he read your letter he said 'I don't understand.' He looked bewildered. Then he said 'What changes is she talking about? What did you do to her?'" He paused.

"Yes? What happened then?"

"Then I gave him your photograph."

"And . . . ?"

"He looked at it for a long time."

"But after that? What did he say then? He must have said something."

For a milli-second Guardian hesitated. Through his retentive and totally accurate memory flashed the incident. Mark had seemed very tense when he had finished reading Olwen's letter, and the hand that had reached out for the photograph had shaken. He had stared at it, and then looked up at Guardian in blank disbelief. "What is *this* supposed to be?"

"It is Olwen, of course."

For a moment Guardian had thought that Mark was going to be sick. "And I . . ." He had stopped and then said between his teeth, "It's some kind of joke, of course. That's it." And Guardian had shaken his head.

After staring at the picture again Mark had said, "*This* is Olwen? This disgusting creature?"

That had stung, and he had snapped back, "She is both functional and beautiful!"

"My god!" Mark had been sweating. His face had turned a dirty grey colour and the sweat beaded his forehead. He had wiped his face with his hands and managed a shaky laugh.

"You know, I had nightmares about this face. Doc said it was just the concussion . . . that it'd wear off. But it's *real*. This is . . . Olwen."

He had pushed the photograph away from him and Guardian had asked, "Do you not wish to keep it?"

Mark had laughed, a coarse forced laugh. "You have to be joking!" So he had picked the photograph off the bed and put it away in his uniform pocket. Then he stood quietly by the bed waiting for Mark to pull himself together.

After a time Mark had looked up. "You still here? What do you want now?"

"I am waiting," he had replied.

"For what?"

"For your answer to Olwen's letter. I must not leave without it. She will be waiting for it."

"Oh, lord!" Mark had said under his breath. Guardian could not tell from the tone if it was a prayer or an expletive. "What am I going to say?" he had appealed, but Guardian had remained silent. "Well, know-it-all, tell me!"

"I cannot write your letter for you, sir. But . . . I warn you . . . do not hurt my Olwen." The words had come out more forcefully than he had expected, and Mark had whitened again and looked rather desperately around the hospital room. It was empty except for the Guardian and himself.

"Don't you threaten me," he had blustered.

"I will not do that," Guardian had agreed, and then amended it. "I *believe* I will not do anything to hurt you."

Mark had grabbed a piece of paper, chewed at the top of his stylo for a minute, and then scribbled a couple of lines. "There. Will that do?"

Guardian had read the note, and then folded it neatly and put it in his pocket. "You are wasted as a farmer, sir. You should have stayed on Earth and become a politician."

"Damn it! What else *could* I write? That I love her? Want her? It's enough. Now get out!" . . .

With Olwen's question ringing in his ears Guardian came to a very human, but for him a momentous decision. He lied. "What did Mark say? Why, he looked at the photograph for a long time and then he said, 'If I could only be like her we could be so happy on Isis.'"

"He wasn't disgusted at the way I am?"

"I told you he would not be. I told you that you are beautiful."

"'If only' . . . that's what he said?"

"Yes. You can understand his feelings. He must always be restricted to the valleys, unless he wears UVO suits and

111

carries cumbersome oxygen equipment. You have the freedom of all Isis. He is proud, and he would never hold you back."

It was a magnificent lie, and he saw its success mirrored in her face. Her expression was tragic, but her self-worth was intact. It was all he could do for her.

But still she would not let go. "If he were to have surgery . . . Guardian, couldn't you . . . ?"

He shook his head. "He is too old for genetic manipulation. The rest would be too difficult. Too painful. His body would try to reverse it. I told you this before—don't you remember?"

"Could you change *me* back?"

"You? Olwen, you would sacrifice your freedom for *him*?"

"Oh, Guardian, it wouldn't be a sacrifice."

Almost he told her how little her hero was worth. He hesitated and then said only, "*I* could not do it. Perhaps, back on Earth, they may have the technology by now."

She sighed then, and let it go; and he left her alone. There were readings to be taken, already overdue.

Olwen sat alone on the terrace, mourning without tears for the might-have-beens of life; and in the next few days she tried to live as she had lived before Pegasus Two, before Mark. She really tried, but the savour had gone. It was not that she was precisely unhappy. It was more as if she were solar-powered and had been too long in the dark.

One morning the feeling became unbearable. She could not sit still, and yet there was nowhere she wished to go, nothing she wanted to do. She paced up and down the terrace, twenty steps to the north, twenty to the south. There was a restless itchy feeling under her skin.

She was still pacing up and down when Guardian hurried out of the house. "I have just computed the approach of another cosmic storm. I have warned the village."

"So soon after the other? Is there anything I can do to help?"

"Stay close to home, that is all. I will let you know when it is time to come into the deep shelter."

She nodded absently, but as he turned to go back into the

112

house, she called to him. "Guardian, it is the strangest thing. I *knew* there was going to be a storm. That is to say, my body knew, only I didn't realise what it was saying. It is just the way it was the last time, when I was up in Bamboo Valley."

He stared at her, and then shook his head slowly. "I put no such capability into you, Olwen. If this is true then you are yourself adapting to Isis, becoming more and more one with the planet. What is this warning like?"

"It's a peculiar kind of restlessness, like an itching underneath my skin. When I felt it that day up north it made me leave the valley and climb up into the mountains as high as I could go, even though I didn't know why."

"And you never felt these sensations before?"

She shook her head. "I wonder . . . perhaps because you were always here, looking after me, telling me what to do, that I paid no attention to how I felt. In Bamboo Valley I was alone, and I had space to listen to my body."

"It is logical. Do you have the same sensations today?"

"Yes. It feels exactly the same. Only it is not quite so intense. I wonder why?"

"Possibly the storm will not be so severe, though my instruments indicate differently. Or perhaps the mountain ranges to the north act as a baffle."

"That makes sense. The storms always come out of the north, and there are two mountain ranges between us and the plain below Bamboo Valley. But Ra is up there." She pointed. "It shines on this valley equally as on the other."

"Perhaps the warning you get does not come from Ra. Perhaps there is something on Isis itself that is communicating with you. It is very interesting. Perhaps . . ." A warning buzzer interrupted his thought and he stopped in midsentence and hurried back into the house.

The wind was beginning to rise, not yet in the valley, but high up, aloft. All morning the sky had been a clear bluegreen. Now it was stained with dark streaks so that it looked like a slab of dull greenish marble, heavy and opaque. As Olwen stood by the balustrade she saw two eagles spiralling slowly down to their eyrie high in the eastern mountains across the river. Suddenly they were thrown sideways, as if buffeted by a huge invisible hand, and smashed against the rock face. She caught her breath and narrowed her eyes to search for them, but they did not rise again.

She turned towards the house. This was going to be a very bad storm. What did that mean, following so closely on the heels of the last? It was almost as if Isis itself was angry at the invasion of the colonists. She felt a twinge of guilt, as if it were her fault. As if her anger and resentment had somehow proved contagious . . . but that was ridiculous.

She left the terrace and in the doorway bumped into Guardian. "One of their young people is missing," he told her.

"Not . . . ?" A hand squeezed her heart so that it hurt physically, as if someone had punched her breast-bone.

"Mark? He is barely mobile. No, it is the littlest one. I do not expect you have even seen him."

The littlest. Olwen had a flash of memory. She saw the village street with the houses all shut against her. She heard her own voice screaming out her hurt and anger at Hobbit's death. She could remember clearly the fear and horror on the faces of them all. All but one. One mischievous dark face with huge brown eyes and a wide grin that flashed white teeth.

"I think . . . what is he like?"

"Five years old . . . that is nine Earth-years. His name is Jody and he is from the highlands of East Africa."

"Only *five*. Out in a storm? Where did he go, Guardian? Do the settlers have any idea? Have they sent out search parties?"

Guardian shook his head. "They have no idea where he went. He was apparently a very curious child, always exploring, getting into scrapes. Captain Tryon says there is to be no search. They can not afford to lose able-bodied men in a search for one child."

"That's terrible. He'll never survive alone." She paced the terrace, hands to her mouth, and then turned, talking quickly. "Guardian, I want you to radio the Captain and ask if anyone, Jody's parents, his friends, *anyone*, knows anything at all about him that might give me a clue where he is. Some place he was particularly curious about, for instance.

114

Somewhere that fascinated him more than any other."

"Why do you wish to know? It is purely academic. You are not thinking of going out yourself, are you? Oh, no, Olwen! I lost your mother and father that way. Not you."

"Quickly." She gave him a push. "Radio the Captain."

After he had gone back to the communications room Olwen stood biting her lip for a minute. Then she too ran, to her own room. A thicker jumpsuit. A cap for her hair and a pair of goggles and a scarf against the sand. Then a quick side trip to the kitchen for a water-bottle and some food. Protein biscuits would do . . . nothing messy. She pushed a handful into her pocket. Oxygen? No, it would weigh her down too much, and the child was too small to climb very high. If he was to be found it would be somewhere down in the valley or on the lower flanks of the mountains.

Her heart sank as she thought of all the places the child might be. The valley was so wide, and shoulder-deep in grass—grass that would probably be more than head-high for a youngster like Jody. If only she could take a floater, get a bird's eye view; but in the winds that would shortly be coming a floater would have no more chance than the eagles.

Guardian came out of the communications room just as she emerged from the kitchen with her supplies. "Nothing useful," he told her. "The only possible clue is that one of Jody's friends remembered that he kept asking how Lost Creek got its name. But they looked around there on their way to the Pegasus. Nothing."

"It will be a place to start from. It will have to do."

"Olwen, you must not go. I beg you not to go. The radiation . . ."

"You made me very strong." She smiled and put her hands on his arms.

"I know. But I do not know if you are strong enough. You have changed and adapted, but you are a human being and not a machine. I cannot predict your safety limits, even if I did remake you."

"We'll have to take that on trust, then, Guardian. Don't argue. I must go."

"Why? What have the settlers ever done for you? I thought . . . you bewilder me."

"Oh." Olwen gave an uncertain laugh. "Perhaps if it had been one of the others I might have chosen to stay in the storm shelter. But Jody . . . Jody is different. You see, he once smiled at me."

"I do not see. That is the most illogical . . ."

"I have to go. I'm the only one who can. I can withstand the dust and radiation far better than you can. Take care. I'll be back, I promise." She stood on tiptoe to kiss his smooth cheek. Then she ran for the terrace, leaving him standing as still as a statue by the kitchen door, one hand to the cheek that she had kissed.

The wind that fifteen minutes before had smashed the high-soaring eagles was tearing out of the north through every ravine and gully. Olwen could feel it tugging at her clothes as she descended the rocky staircase to the Cascades, and it picked up the falling water and threw it in sudden whirls of spray that made the rocks horribly slippery and the visibility next to nil. She had to make her way several hundred metres down river before the air was clear enough for her to use the binoculars she had brought with her.

With her back against a steadying rock she raked the whole northern end of the valley, both banks of the river, and the lower flanks of the eastern mountains. Nothing moved anywhere, except the thorn bushes, which quivered as the wind tore through their grey branches. Now and then one was torn away from the shallow soil and bowled over and over in a whirl of savage silver thorns until it met an obstacle and stuck there. But of Jody there was no sign.

She set off as fast as she dared along the western bank of the river, close to the steep side of the mesa. Every hundred metres or so she stopped and looked through the glasses again, and shouted the boy's name. She listened, her heart thumping, but there was nothing but the dry cracking of thorn bushes and the giant strum of the wind in the struts of the great Light up on the top of the mesa.

She ran on, balancing on loose scree, leaping sure-footedly from rock slab to rock slab. A kilometre from the Cascades the valley widened out into the bottom grassland. Far over to the right she could see the squat bulk of Pegasus Two. Nothing stirred over there but the flattened grass. The

116

settlers were battened down inside to wait out the storm.

By the time she had reached the western shore of the lake the normally smooth waters were being whipped into short choppy waves, and now and then an extra vicious gust would blow the tops off them in a flurry of grey spume. Beyond the lake the village was deserted. Or so it seemed. Olwen decided that if she did not find Jody along the creek she would return home that way. After all, he might have back-tracked after the settlers had left. Suppose he was right now hiding under a bed, or in a storage unit . . . She began to wish that she had come the other way, along the eastern shore. But on the other hand, she had a better view of the whole valley from this side of the lake.

She pounded through the fruit groves. Much of the fruit, barely formed, had already been shaken from the trees, and the stone-like green knobs bruised her feet as she ran through the grass. At the far end of the grove she stopped to shout Jody's name again, but the wind snatched her voice and stretched it out into a high thin sound like a violin string. After that she did not waste any more time or breath in shouting, but ploughed on downstream towards the mysterious spot where Lost Creek vanished among the rocks.

She remembered the fascination that the spot had had on her when she was Jody's age. All that water, pouring downriver from the Cascades, day after day, year after year, and vanishing into a hole in the ground, just like that. Once, she remembered, she had worked out very logically that when the hole was completely filled with water it would start to overflow and fill up the whole valley. It would climb and climb up the sides of the mountains, like the water in a bathtub, until Isis was completely drowned. She used to go down from the mesa every day to make sure that the hole had not filled up yet. Then she began to have bad dreams about it, and when Guardian found out what it was all about he explained very carefully that the water did not just sit there under the ground, but worked its way through fissures and faults, finally to burst out in half a dozen springs on the far slopes of the southern mountains, to become the rivers of other distant valleys.

Did Jody have the same fantasy? Would she find him lying

117

on his tummy, chin propped on hands, watching the water slide in a solid glassy curve into the hole in the ground? So clear was this picture in her mind that when she finally reached the spot and there was nobody there she could not believe it, but tore off her goggles, blinked her eyes and tried to clean the caked sand from the glass.

She looked north for a moment, into the wind. There was really very little time left, if she was to be of any use, if it was not to be just a lifeless body that she would return to the settlers. She stood tall against the wind and raked the grassland, the southern slopes, the southeast, with the binoculars. Jody wore a red jumpsuit, she had been told. It should show up even more brightly than the settlers' survey stakes. But there was no smudge of red anywhere. Everything was washed over in slate grey and dark foreboding purple.

She lowered the glasses and tried to imagine how she would behave if she were the five-year-old Jody. She squatted by the river, trying to shrink inside her mind from her full-grown body, to be once more small, curious, afraid . . .

If Jody *had* been exploring down here at the end of Lost Creek what would he have noticed first? The wind? The sudden darkening of Ra's light as the clouds and high-borne dust swept across the sky like a curtain. Would he have noticed the changing colours of the landscape and realized that something was wrong? Why hadn't he run home? There would have been time enough. There *should* have been time enough. Unless he hadn't seen what was happening. Unless he had been side-tracked by something else, something much more interesting.

Olwen stared around. She had not been at this end of the valley in ages. Had anything changed? When she squatted down she became aware of shadows beyond the hole through which the river poured. When she stood up the shadows had vanished. That was something a child would notice, a curious child. She walked cautiously across the rough ground towards the biggest shadow, and nearly fell as her feet unexpectedly shot out from under her on a sudden slope of scree. She caught her balance and squatted again. She could hear the rattle of the stones she had dislodged. The sound seemed to go on for a long time. Then there was nothing but the savage wind screaming.

No. There *was* something else. The faint sound of running water. Not from Lost Creek. From a dry hole in the ground, a hole that she had nearly shot down feet first. The sort of hole that might have been made by a large burrowing animal, only there were no burrowing animals that large down in the valley.

Not down there, Jody. Please God, don't let him be down there.

She had brought neither lights nor rope and there was no time to go back for either. The best she could do was to lie on her stomach and wriggle forward into the awful hole until the constriction around her shoulders warned her to stop before she herself got stuck. She yelled, and was nearly deafened by the echo of her voice. She waved her arms about in front of her like a blind swimmer. There was nothing. Only sand and rock and black space.

She kicked and wriggled her way back in a sudden suffocating panic, and scrambled to her feet, coughing and shuddering. There were more holes. The whole area was pock-marked with them, she could see, now that she knew how to look for them. Some were tiny, some almost as big as the one she had just explored. Whatever it was had happened recently. Perhaps it was a sudden collapse of sedimentary rocks into some inner vault, leaving behind the old harder volcanic rock, riddled with vent-holes. It was down one of these that the river flowed. All these other vents, blocked for who knows how many centuries by deposits from the plain, had suddenly been shaken clear.

Why hadn't she known about it? This was her Isis and she had not known. Here was a horrible danger within walking distance of the smallest of the new settlers, and she hadn't been aware of it, hadn't been able to warn them. Neither had Guardian, which was as startling. Guardian knew everything, or so it had always seemed. But, to be fair, he had had a whole planet to map, weather reports to collate, flora and fauna to observe and classify. It was a huge job for one person, even for such a one as Guardian. There should have been her mother and father too, she remembered. And anyway, the more she looked at the holes, the more sure she

119

was that they *were* newly made.

One by one she explored the larger sink-holes, wriggling into each as far as she dared, thrusting her arms into those that were too small for her body. At the fourth she saw a sign. It was a tag of red, no more than a couple of threads, caught on a patch of thorn. She dropped onto her front. It was getting so dark, it might almost be night. Was that another patch of red, looped over a spur of rock? She stretched forward into the dark and felt warm flesh. The tag was the cuff of the child's jumpsuit, torn and caught on a rock spur. She could feel the sole of one foot. Just one foot.

She wriggled forward until her shoulders protested and felt around in the darkness for the other foot. There it was, doubled under the child's knee. Carefully she pulled. Oh, please let nothing catch. Let him come free. She wriggled back, knelt, leaned back pulling, and then reached forward quickly to catch him by the knees. Come on now! Something caught, and she tugged frantically, praying it was clothing and not the boy. She leaned back again, and then there was a sudden rush and noise of stones pouring down the hole, and she was sitting on the verge with a grubby warm bundle in her arms.

Was he alive? If only Guardian were here to help. If only she knew what to do now. He *felt* alive. He didn't feel the way Hobbit had felt when she had held him in her arms. She remembered the water-bottle and carefully washed the child's face. She wet a corner of her scarf and let the water trickle into his mouth. Just a little. Then a little more.

Quite suddenly he stirred and choked. Then he sneezed, a common-place very much alive sneeze. She held him close, feeling the warmth of the little body against hers, and she let the tears run down her face. It didn't matter. There was no one to see. She cried, not just because he was alive, but from a mixture of memories and instincts. She crooned to him and rocked gently to and fro while the tears ran down her face and the whipping sand stuck to them.

But not for long. She felt him struggle in her arms and she let him go. He turned and stared up at her. "Oh, hullo. You're the funny lady!"

"Yes, that's me, all right." Olwen gave a hiccup that was

half laughter, half tears. "Are you hurt?"

He shook his head, "Just awfully thirsty. Hungry too."

"You can have a drink of water and a protein biscuit. Quickly. We're going to have to hurry to get to shelter."

He drank thirstily and wolfed down all the biscuits she had brought. "I was scared," he told her in a whisper that was full of crumbs. "But don't tell the others."

"All right. I won't. What were you doing?"

"Exploring. Everyone's always telling me that I'm too small to build houses or chop down trees or hunt or do anything exciting like that. All I ever get to do is to help in the kitchen, washing up and helping with the vegetables and stuff like that. So today I just decided that I was going to do some exploring on my own. It was great too. Only something happened and I got stuck. I couldn't get back and I couldn't go forward. And nobody came. Not for hours and hours." His chin suddenly wobbled and Olwen gave him a consoling hug and got to her feet.

"That's because nobody knew where you had gone. The first rule, especially for explorers on strange planets, is to tell somebody else where they are going."

"I see that now. Only if I'd told them they wouldn't have let me go." He sighed heavily.

"Well, it's all over now. And you did make an important discovery, something even I didn't know about. Now I know you're too big really, but the storm's getting worse and we're going to have to hurry, so you're going to ride piggyback, all right?"

She put her goggles on Jody's face, and wrapped her scarf over his mouth. "Now get your legs around my waist and hold onto my shoulders like mad. Don't let go. I'm going to run." She jolted him into position, got a firm grip on his knees and set out.

Jody was not heavy, but the wind was sweeping down from the northern mountains to east and west of the mesa, so that across the valley it buffeted her first from one direction, then from the other. The noise was overwhelming, and the sharp-leaved grasses slashed at her thick jumpsuit as she ran. She feared for Jody's legs, but she dared not stop.

She set a straight line across the plain for the outline of

121

Pegasus Two, and she ran steadily, pushing aside grass, going over knolls and protruding rocks, straight towards the burnt circle of grass in the centre of the plain.

She fell twice, each time jolting the breath from her body and bruising her knees. But she still kept her grip on Jody, and he, like a baby hobbit, kept his hands twisted tightly in the fabric of her suit. Without the goggles her eyes quickly filled with sand. Against this particular problem her nictating membranes were worse than useless. Tiny particles of sand lodged between the two layers and caused her additional pain.

She ran on, head down, dazed by the noise and the wind that continually hit at her with fists that seemed real and solid, until her body ached. When she finally burst out of the long grass into the circle of burnt-off stubble, now silver with fresh young shoots, she was not aware of it, but ran blindly on until she smacked into one of the great angled feet that supported the space ship on the ground.

She blinked through her streaming eyes. She could hardly see at all. Was that the stairway at the far side? She groped forward, felt rungs under her feet.

She would need her hands to climb. "Hold on tight, Jody. Hold on with your legs as well," she shouted at him, and began the perilous climb to the entrance of the ship.

The wind was her enemy. It dragged her back every time she loosened her grip to reach up to the next rung. It tore and beat at her. But still she would not let go, and still Jody clung to her back. Twenty rungs. Twenty times to fight, reach out and win.

There was the door at last. With the very last gram of energy in her body she hung onto the railing with her left hand and with her right fist pounded on the closed door. Pounded and pounded again.

Chapter Ten

Inside the space ship it was stiflingly hot, and after the first hour the air began to feel solid, thick and used up. Some sort of air-cooler and circulator had been hooked up to the solar batteries for just such an emergency. Olwen could hear the thud-thud of the pump above the restless movement of bodies and the anxious low-voiced conversations. Only it simply was not enough for the needs of eighty lively settlers plus the crew. On the long voyage from Earth, after all, the settlers had been in hypno-sleep, their oxygen requirements minimal, their body heat lowered to hibernation temperatures.

When the outer door had first been opened in response to Olwen's frantic knocking Jody had been snatched from her shoulders, hugged, patted, consoled. She herself had begun to descend the ladder, prepared to battle the storm across the grassland and up the valley to home. Only they had not allowed her to. She had been pulled into the ship by eager hands. She too had been hugged and thanked in a sudden joyful release of the settlers' anxiety over Jody. For a wonderful moment she felt the warmth, the sense of belonging.

But then it began to change. First the laughter and the loud voices had died down. They had drawn back, uneasily, until in the crowded central section of the ship there was a space of a metre all round her. There was no more conversation, but an uncomfortable silence. Olwen backed herself into a corner in the shadow of a bulkhead and squatted down on the floor. Her head was spinning and her ears ringing with the silence that had followed the incessant scream of the wind. She licked her dry lips and let her sore eyes shut. Suddenly she felt old and tired.

A dark woman with eyes like Jody's came and knelt beside her, silently offering her a glass of water. She drank most of it and tried to wash the sand from her eyes with the rest. As she gave the glass back Jody, now completely recovered and as rambunctious as ever, hurled himself onto Olwen's lap and gave her a wet noisy kiss.

Olwen felt the horrified withdrawal of the others as clearly as she could hear Jody's mother's faint indrawn hiss of distress. For a moment she held the compact muscular little body against her heart. Then she pushed him gently away, and tried to make herself small in the shadowed corner. After a while she pretended to be asleep, and felt the sudden easing of the tension around her.

She kept her eyes shut, and never once allowed herself to look around for Mark. The air grew even heavier. It smelt of dust and sweat and anxiety. Even the settlers were beginning to complain, and Olwen was almost in a stupor, before word came to the Captain from Guardian that the storm had passed and they might safely leave their shelter.

As soon as two of the crew had undogged the big door Olwen slipped out and down the ladder into the comparative freshness of the air outside. In the cheerful buzz of conversation and the milling around that followed the Captain's announcement her action was not even noticed, except by Jody. He pulled at his mother's jacket.

"She's gone." His face puckered up and his lower lip stuck out in a little shelf.

"If you leave your lip out you'll likely trip over it. Who's she? . . . the cat's grandmother?"

"The funny lady. She's gone and I didn't even say goodbye."

"Oh." Jody's mother stopped talking and looked confused and embarrassed. "Oh, well, I guess she was just in a hurry to get home where she belongs, Jody."

"But I wanted to talk to her again."

"Poor girl," the other woman said to Jody's mother over his head. "Can you imagine going through life looking like that."

"Like Hallowe'en," Jody interrupted, and laughed, teeth and eyes shining in his black face. "She's fun."

124

"Oh, hush up!" His mother put a hand over his mouth and laughed nervously.

"He's just too young to understand, that's all," the other woman comforted her confusion.

Mark heard them. Ever since he realised that it was Olwen who had rescued Jody, and that she was still aboard, he had been in dread of seeing her. Because of his invalid status he had been allotted a couch in a corner, and he had lain with his eyes shut, afraid that if he opened them for an instant he might see her standing there in front of him . . . accusingly. He was ashamed of himself and angry at Olwen and the Guardian for having got him into such an embarrassing predicament. The memories that his mind had denied him when he was ill now returned again and again.

It was like an obsessive dream. Over and over he saw the drift of gauzy stuff she had been wearing, the floating red hair, cracklingly alive under the blue-white light of Ra. Over and over he saw her turn in a swirl of fabric and hair that swung back to reveal the nightmare features they had hidden. Every time he remembered the scene he felt the same inward lurch of surprise and disgust. It was as if he had plucked a beautiful rose and in the instant that he lifted it to his face to smell its scent, it had turned into a snake.

Even while he shuddered, the rational part of Mark's mind admitted that if he had first met Olwen as a member of an alien species he would have approached her with nothing more than scientific interest. He would have admired her body for its serviceability on Isis. He might even have acknowledged it as beautiful, as one might consider a lizard beautiful, or a tropical fish. Certainly the contrast of green-bronze skin with the lustrous blue of her eyes and the flaming red of her hair was stunning. But as a person? As a human being?

He asked himself why he felt so ashamed. He had walked with her, hand in hand. He had shared his inmost thoughts about life and poetry and God and music. And, to be just, she had shared hers with him . . . but not the main fact. Not the fact of her inhuman appearance. Why hadn't she told him

125

that? Why had she hidden behind that insipidly pretty Anglo-Saxon mask? She had cheated him.

It had not been his fault—none of it. From first to last it was she who had made a fool out of *him*, who had trapped *him* into loving her. He had kept his anger hot. It helped keep the pain away and blotted out the sense of betrayal that niggled at his conscience in the night hours when his ribs ached and he could not sleep. Because he had to hate. To be angry. Because he could not go on loving Olwen. Not possibly. Not ever.

Then he had heard the two women and Jody talking about her, and for an instant the shame was almost too much to bear. Then, after the shame, came a sense of reprieve, as if someone had lifted a weight off his chest. She had gone back to the mesa where she belonged. He was not going to have to see her, to face her and face the reproach that he knew was his due. She had gone.

Suddenly he pushed himself off his couch and limped stiffly through the crowd towards the door. Everyone was eager to be off the stuffy ship and get back to the village to see what damage the storm had done; and he got several painful jabs in his still tender ribs as he fought his way to the door.

The false night had blown away, and Ra shone low in the west, sending long mountain shadows chasing across the grassland. The tattered remnants of the storm still tossed the grasses, flattening them suddenly, and as suddenly letting them go, so that the valley was filled with a movement of silver and rose.

Beyond this silvery sea Mark could see Olwen. She had already reached the stone-strewn flanks of the mesa. At this distance he could see only the silver of her jumpsuit and the red of her hair. He felt a sudden pain in his chest, as if his ribs had been broken again, and a deep sense of desolation. She was running hard, running from *him*.

He found that he was shouting her name. It was not any good. The wind that still blew fitfully from the north picked up her name and tore it apart. He clutched the railing at the top of the stairway and stared after the small silver figure.

"Do you *mind*?" An irascible voice behind him made him

jump and turn. "The way you pushed and shoved I thought you were in a hurry. If you're going to moon around all day please let me by."

By the time Mark had apologized and scrambled down the stairway Olwen had gone. The mesa brooded, a great shape dominating the grassland to the north, the spidery filaments of the Light catching the last gleams of the sun. Mark walked slowly back to the village, numb with an inexplicable loss.

On the day after the storm Captain Tryon paid a formal call on Olwen. He waited until evening, when the ultraviolet radiation from Ra would be minimal, and he wore his dress uniform with its gold star-and-galaxy insignia, and he carried only a small oxygen outfit in his side pocket.

Olwen, too, recognised the formality of the occasion. With a deliberate sense of the pattern of destiny she wore, for the second time only since her birthday, the musical dress that Guardian had made for her. That day had become a watershed in her life. When she looked back she could see all the days before that day as a time of carefree childhood, culminating in Guardian's beautiful gift. Then had come the message from Pegasus Two, and nothing had been the same since, nor could it be. Isis was no longer her playground, and she herself was no more than a pensioner of STC. Her sense of her own worth had been totally destroyed . . . no, she told herself with meticulous truth, not destroyed, or why should she be dressing so carefully for this visit from the Captain? But it had been badly damaged.

She could hear the Captain's deep voice talking to Guardian in the living room. Guardian would make him comfortable and give him a drink. She need not hurry. Deliberately she slid the shining golden folds over her head and settled them carefully. She had dressed her hair high on top of her head in a new style that she felt fitted her adult self. She just hoped that it wouldn't fall down. She could ask Guardian to help her with it, but no, that seemed to belong to the other side of her, the child side, that she had left behind.

There was a pain deep inside her, but she bore it proudly.

You are a woman, not a child, she told herself, and with her head high she walked slowly down the passage to the living room.

She startled the daylights out of Captain Tryon. She could not know that her sudden appearance from among the shadows reminded him of some exotic goddess. All she could see was that he was impressed by her appearance. He jumped to his feet and put his glass down blindly, without looking, without taking his eyes off her.

To be an adult and to hide one's hurt is rather like acting in a play, thought Olwen, as she walked slowly across the room and seated herself with studied grace in the chair opposite the Captain's. She bowed her head slightly in acknowledgement of his presence and indicated with a wave of her hand that he might sit again.

The music in her dress was low and minor-key today, and it whispered into silence as she sat, very still, waiting for what the Captain had to say.

He cleared his throat in the silence. "Miss Pendennis, I have to come to thank you on behalf of Jody's parents, and indeed the whole settlement, for saving Jody's life. His mother and father truly wanted to come with me to thank you in person, but we felt that we should respect your wishes, and that I alone should be your contact with the village. Though if you would consider changing your mind . . ."

Olwen made a sudden movement and her dress jangled discordantly. Captain Tryon looked at her expectantly, but she sat back quietly in her chair again, her dress shivering into stillness. After a moment he went on. "We have been appallingly insensitive to you. We would like you to try and forgive us and perhaps understand. The unknown, the unexpected, can sometimes be very shocking."

"Perhaps I am . . . shocking."

"Not to Jody. He hasn't stopped talking about you."

Olwen smiled faintly. "Jody is still young enough not to be prejudiced."

"Jody is lucky. Perhaps, if you could understand . . . your upbringing here must have been so different . . . but on Earth we grow up surrounded by fears and prejudices that we

128

hardly recognise or understand ourselves. 'Oh, look, a spider. Squash it!' An instant thoughtless reaction to the unexpected."

"Am *I* like a spider to you?"

"Of course not! That was just an example." Captain Tryon's laugh seemed spontaneous, but was it perhaps too hearty? Did it go on just a little too long?

"What am I like?"

"Can you not accept that you are just yourself Olwen Pendennis, the Keeper of the Isis Light?"

"Oh, yes, of course. That's easy for me to accept. But can *you*?"

There was silence for a while. The Captain turned to the window, looking up at the stars pricking out in the sky above the dark bulk of the eastern mountains. "Forgive me," he said at last. "We have a long way to go and a lot to learn and unlearn."

She nodded her head. After a while he turned to look at her again. "I believe I told you that we intend to hollow out caves at the bottom of the south side of the mesa. Your . . . Guardian can help us with that."

"Will you abandon your village by the lake then?"

"No. But the settlers need a safe storage for sensitive equipment, and storm shelters during solar flares."

"I can appreciate that. Pegasus Two was not precisely comfortable."

"Not only that. We will not always be here, you realise. Once the settlement is well established my crew and I return to Earth."

"What will you do then?"

"Pick up another group of settlers. Perhaps we may return to Isis. More probably we will be directed to some other planet."

"Is Earth really *that* overcrowded?"

"Crowded and worked out and damaged. We've made too many mistakes. We have to start over. Start better, in as many places as we can."

"What a pity that the prejudices cannot be left behind when you go into star-drive."

There was a silence. The Captain looked blankly out at the

stars. After a while Olwen said quietly, "Was that all, Captain?"

"There is one more matter." He spoke uneasily.

"You have my attention."

"It is an idea of Doctor MacDonald's. If you would like . . . if you would consider going back to Earth with us, it is possible that with Earth technology we might be able to undo what your Guardian did to you."

"What exactly do you mean?"

"We could change you back. Make you like—us."

"And afterwards? Could you bring me back to Isis? It is my home, you realise."

"It could probably be arranged, if you wished it."

Olwen stared at the Captain. She had made the same suggestion to Guardian, weeks before, when she had received Mark's first letter. Then it had seemed to be a possible way of making Mark love her. Now . . . "I think you mean well, but you don't really understand what you are saying. It is an outrageous idea to come from you. If you inhabited a world and a colony of tongueless people landed, would you consent to having your tongue cut out so that you could be like them?"

"That's a disgusting comparison!"

"It's a disgusting idea. Captain, this is *my* planet. I am safe wherever I go, in upper or lower Isis. The air is good for me. The ultra-violet doesn't harm me. I am immune to stings and bites. Should I become like your settlers, grovelling in the valley, all the beauty of upper Isis shut off from me for ever?"

"Things will change. The atmosphere will be enriched eventually. The ionosphere will become more dense."

"That will take generations and you know it. *Now* Isis is mine."

"Very well. Forgive me if I insulted you. It was only a suggestion. But won't you consider coming down from your isolation and making your home with us?"

"Why?"

"Living alone is not healthy for body or mind. As you get older . . ."

"Alone? Have you forgotten Guardian? I have never been

130

alone. Guardian has been mother and father and friend and teacher and counsellor. I don't need any of you, Captain Tryon." Olwen jumped to her feet in a torrent of sound.

"Good grief, Miss Pendennis, you talk of your so-called Guardian as if he were Jehovah. He's only a damned robot, after all!" The Captain's temper snapped. It had been a difficult interview.

She stood and stared at him. "You're crazy!"

"Oh, come on. Stop playing games. Enough is enough. You can see with your own eyes . . . and what about the original manifest for setting up the Isis Light? Keepers Gareth and Liz Pendennis and one robot—DaCoP Forty-three."

"Day Cop?" Olwen asked faintly. Had she gone mad? Or had Captain Tryon?

"Data Collector and Processor. DaCoP."

"You're crazy." She shook her head. "Go. At once. Please." She stood straight and still, holding on to the back of the sofa, staring past him with her strangely beautiful eyes. Captain Tryon opened his mouth to say something more, then shrugged, bowed and went out onto the terrace. So he'd muffed it. Phil MacDonald had bet him that he would, and the good doctor was right as usual, blast it.

Olwen stood as straight as a golden shaft of bamboo until the sound of the Captain's floater had faded into the silence of the Isis night. She felt abandoned, alone. Then, unexpectedly, *not* alone, as she turned to see Guardian standing close beside her.

She looked up into the dear familiar face and saw him, in a dizzy unreal flash, as Captain Tryon and the others must see him. She sat down abruptly in a discord of music, feeling suddenly faint and sick.

Guardian moved swiftly, brought her a drink, stood over her while she sipped it. "Thank you." When she handed him the empty glass her hands were trembling. She could not look at him. She felt as if she were in the presence of a complete stranger.

"Olwen!" His voice commanded.

"Yes, Guardian?"

131

"Please look at me."

She raised her eyes reluctantly and saw him as he had always been, her dear comfortable constant friend. She smiled with relief and put her hands in his. "I don't understand. Am I seeing you as you are, or as you want me to see you? Which is real?"

"It's quite simple. To you I am Guardian, as I have always been. Captain Tryon can only see DaCoP Forty-three."

"But which are you *really*?"

"Both. There is no difficulty."

Olwen put her hands to her head and laughed weakly. "No? But you . . . instead of my mother . . . I thought you loved me."

"I do, Olwen. Haven't I always cared for you and protected you and taught you?"

"Y-yes."

"Isn't that loving?"

"I don't know . . . I suppose so. Guardian, when I was little you used to rock me on your knee."

"You still remember that?"

"Oh, yes. I remember feeling warm and secure and loved. Guardian, what did you feel, when you were holding me like that?"

"Feel? I thought about your mother and tried to put those thoughts into you," he said simply.

She nodded, unable to speak. Then she got up and kissed the smooth cheek of her old friend and walked in a gentle cadence of sound along the passage to her own room.

When Ra rose above the eastern mountains its first silver beams caught her hair as she sat motionless by her window. She had shed the golden dress. It lay in a mute heap on the floor, and she was wrapped in a warm sleeping robe. She had sat all night by the window, watching the stars. She had remembered many things, thought out many ideas, and come to a single decision.

But first, she must see Mark once more, if that were possible. She had to lay this one ghost, or it would come back to haunt her decision. She was not hungry, but her sleepless night had made her a little light-headed, so that her move-

132

ments were slower than usual. She showered and picked at random a jumpsuit to wear.

Out on the terrace, still chilly from the night, she hesitated, wondering whether to take a floater or not. But she was in no hurry, and in the end she decided to walk. She climbed down the stone stairs beside the Cascades and stood for a moment, watching the rainbows of gold, green, blue and purple, that hovered, vanished and reappeared among the spray. It had never looked so beautiful.

After a while she walked slowly downstream towards the village. She did not go right in, but stopped about five hundred metres away, and sat down on a flat slab of rock that overhung the river. The settlers had seen her. She was aware of it without having to turn round and look. It was like a kind of uneasy electricity. They left her alone, all except the irrepressible Jody.

"Hi, funny lady!"

"Hullo, Jody. How are you?"

"Fine." He scrambled onto the rocks beside her and sat, kicking his heels. The fishes that had been lurking in the quiet shadow under the rock darted suddenly away.

"My father wopped me for going off on my own that day," he said after a while.

"Oh, I'm sorry."

Jody shrugged. "Didn't hurt much. And Mom said it was just because he cared."

"I'm sure that's true. You won't go off by yourself again, will you?"

"No, sir!" He rolled his dark eyes at her. "You mightn't be around next time."

"No. I don't suppose I will," Olwen said slowly. "Jody, will you do something for me?"

"Sure."

"Go and ask Mark if he will come and talk with me?"

"Okay." Jody scrambled to his feet and tore back along the stony path to the village.

Olwen saw him talk to his mother. Heard someone call. Then another voice answered from inside one of the houses. It seemed a long time before a tall familiar figure emerged from one of the houses and began to walk stiffly towards her.

She stared down into the river. She dug her nails into the palms of her hands. The fishes were back in the quiet shadow under the stone. She heard a scrunch of gravel. She could feel him behind her, feel the closeness as he sat down on the sun-warmed rock. Suddenly she could not breathe, and she had forgotten her carefully worded speech.

From a long way off she heard his voice. "I didn't think you would ever want to see me again."

"Just once more." She swallowed. Did her voice sound normal to him? "It seemed fitting that I should come to say goodbye."

"*Goodbye*? Where are you going?"

She shrugged, holding the tears at bay with a smile. "To an upland valley I know, several days to the north by floater."

"You're going to live there?"

"Yes."

"*Alone*?"

"I won't be alone. I have Guardian."

"But . . ."

"Guardian was all I ever had. And before you came I was never lonely or sad for a minute." She looked directly at him then, so that she saw several tiny Marks, all glistening and moving in the shimmer of her tears.

"When you left the ship," he said after a while. "I had the feeling that it was me you were running away from."

"It was," she interrupted.

". . . and I felt abandoned," he went on. And then stared. "You *were* running away from me? Why?"

"Oh, Mark, you are so stupid! Because I can't bear to be close to you. Because I can't spend the rest of my life looking down on the valley where you live."

"I wish you wouldn't go," he said slowly. "I don't understand why I feel that, Olwen. But it's true."

She shrugged and made herself laugh. "Too bad. I'm going."

"But . . ." He stopped and shook his head. "I *love* you." When he said it, it was as if he had diagnosed the illness that had caused his weariness and lack of appetite.

"How can you love me, Mark, when you can't even bear to look at me?"

134

"I *can*." His profile was towards her. She saw his throat move as he swallowed. "I know now that I do love you. The real you. Inside. Not what your . . . what Guardian did to you. That'd take a bit of getting used to. But I will, Olwen." He turned and faced her, his mouth firm, his eyes full of such resolve that her heart skipped in her chest.

It was hard to smile when his eyes were on her. "Well, you're growing up," she teased softly. "But it's no good, Mark. We mustn't play games. We have nothing in common, not even the same appearance of humanity. Isis is mine, from the valleys to the mountain peaks, summer and winter and cosmic storm. You can't share that with me and I will not spend my life as a prisoner. I must be free." Her lips were so dry that she could hardly say the last words. For a second she let herself put her arms around him, not looking at the expression on his face. Then she turned her back and ran all the way up the valley to the Cascades.

"Why did you do it?" Guardian asked her later, when she had finished crying and told him what she had said.

"It had to be finished between us for ever," she explained. "Or he would have carried around that guilt and it would have spoiled things for him. I hope he'll be all right now. I expect he'll marry one of the settler girls and they'll raise a family and be happy. I'll be nothing but a funny memory. It must be that way."

"What about you, Olwen? Can you be happy?"

She did not answer him directly. She stared into the distance, and then said softly, "When I saw his face I knew there was no possibility, not even a crumb of hope. He felt so guilty, and he tried so hard not to show how he felt. It's not his fault."

"It was mine. Oh, Olwen, I am so sorry."

"It's no one's fault. Guardian. Where is your logic? You did what you had to for my own good. You gave me a great gift, the freedom of a planet. Was there ever anything more grand? I'm grateful, dear Guardian. Truly."

"Is there *anything* I can do?"

"Yes. I want you to make us a new home, in the mountain

135

above that upland valley where the giant bamboos grow. Little Hobbit is there. He'll be waiting for me. And I've been thinking. I can still be useful to the settlers up there. The other side of the range is much closer to the northern storms. Remember my built-in warning system? I can tell you when I 'feel' a cosmic storm brewing before even your instruments do. Then you can radio a warning to the settlers. I'd like to feel useful. To be part of them, just a little."

"The Light?"

"Is nothing that they cannot handle, if you show them. Now that a colony is established here there is only the shipping signal, and that is practically automatic."

"That is true. We can go as soon as I have lasered out storm shelters for the settlers. Olwen, are you sure?"

"Very, very sure."

"You won't be lonely?"

"Less lonely than I would be if I stayed here. And I'll have you. Oh, Guardian, you won't go and die before I do, will you?"

"Of course not. What an idea! We DaCoPs are built to last."

"Good. That's settled then." She blew her nose and got to her feet. "Guardian, I'm starving. Isn't that funny, after all this? Can you find me something nice to eat?"

Later, when she had finished a very late breakfast, Olwen looked across at the golden figure of Guardian and felt a sudden surge of tenderness towards him. "Oh, Guardian!"

"What's the matter?"

"Nothing. I love you. But I just realised something so sad. When I die, then *you* will be all alone. *You* will have no one."

"That is all right, Olwen. You must not be distressed. After all, I am not human. DaCoPs do not have the capacity to be lonely."

Olwen nodded and watched him walk stiffly across the living room to the kitchen.

"Poor Guardian," she whispered.